ADVANCED PRAISE FOR CATFISHED

Well written with an entertaining storyline that has the right amount of mystery and romance. This is one of those series that you just know will be a huge hit. I will be impatiently waiting for the next adventure with Rylie!

— SUSAN C. (NETGALLEY REVIEWER)

Catfished had me laughing out loud.

— HEIDI W. (NETGALLEY REVIEWER)

I enjoyed this light-hearted story very much. The main character is very relatable and as a reader, I connected well with all of her situations and experiences. With the sweet mix of romance, comedy, and mystery I loved the characters and how the story was put together. I can not wait til the next book in the series to find out what happens to this character!

— LINDSAY B. (NETGALLEY EDUCATOR)

D1226002

What a funny and witty mystery! Catfished has the makings of a wonderful mystery series! Rylie Cooper has captured my attention as a heroine in training.

A great cast of characters, this story was quick to grab my interest and had moments that really made me smile. I look forward to more stories about Rylie, Luke and the entire gang!

Such a fun read that literally had me laughing out loud! I am definitely going to continue reading the Rylie Cooper mysteries, if more are to come! A fun, easy read for anyone! I loved the suspense, love, and of course die hard laughter thrown throughout the book!

CATFISHED

A RYLIE COOPER MYSTERY

STELLA BIXBY

FERRY TAIL PUBLISHING LLC

For my amazing family. I love you.

S tress breakout. Perfect. The nasty pimple on my chin peered back at me from my rearview mirror. There was no way I could walk into an interview with that monster on my face. I caked on foundation as thick as the dust on the back of my TV in an attempt to cover it.

Deep breath in . . . and out. Living back with my parents was temporary. Was I thankful to have a place to stay after my entire life had practically collapsed in on itself a week ago? Absolutely. Had I ever thought I'd be one of *those* kids who returned to their parents' basement as an adult? Not in a million years.

I was a college educated, hard-working, independent woman. All I needed now was a job. Five interviews in four days and not so much as a "we've gone in another direction" phone call. Not a great track record. But sixth time's the charm, right?

My father had found the ad in the morning newspaper.

The front page featured a grainy photo of Ronnie Tilsdale holding his state-record catfish—a slimy, whiskered blob almost as big as Ronnie himself.

At the end of the story, the report noted that Prairie City, the fifth largest city in Colorado, was looking for summer urban park rangers. Urban park rangers? What did they do? Defend the homeless from murderers, drug dealers, and rabid dogs? If not for the required degree in Parks and Recreation Management, I'd have probably skipped right over the ad, but seeing as how that was exactly the degree I held, I submitted an application and received a call back the next day for an interview. Bring on the murderers.

Opening the door of Cherry Anne, my red Mustang now one payment shy of repossession, I tugged my skirt down and made sure the pantyhose my mother had *insisted* I wear hadn't formed a static electricity alliance with the hem. I squared my shoulders and steadied myself on my heels, doing my best impression of a runway walk. In my mind I looked like Alessandra Ambrosio or Giselle Bundchen, but in reality I'm sure I looked more like a flamingo on roller skates.

When I walked into the large tiki-style building on the edge of the Alder Ridge Reservoir, a pretty woman with gigantic blonde 80's hair smiled at me but continued to listen to a weasel-like man's complaint.

"He caught that fish illegally, Car," the lanky man said, his face turning an ugly shade of fuchsia above his stringy beard. "He better watch his back or he'll end up in the same predicament as that fish he caught—dead."

"You can't just go around making threats like that over

a stupid fish, Dave." Her shirt showed more cleavage than Dolly Parton. "And I've already told you, the rangers are looking into it."

Dave muttered something about pansy-ass rangers and marched out of the office bumping my shoulder on his way.

"What can I do for ya?" She smacked her bubble gum.

I regained my composure—forcing myself not to yell 'excuse you' after him—and smiled as sweetly as I could. "I'm here for an interview."

"We're not doing any more interviews for receptionist. Maybe you were supposed to go to the City Offices?"

The pantyhose were definitely too much. "I'm here for the summer park ranger position."

"Oh, you must be Rylie." She looked me up and down. "The guys are gonna love you." She giggled.

I shifted from one foot to another. I had gotten the same reaction when I joined the fire department.

"Let me see where they're at." She picked up a mic attached to a radio base station mounted under her desk. "Office One to Ranger Four."

She stuck a long, manicured finger into her mouth and pulled out a string of bright pink gum. After she twirled it around and around, she scraped it back into her mouth with her crooked teeth.

"Ranger Four, go ahead," a deep voice came back through the speaker.

"Yeah, I got Rylie here to interview for the summer ranger position."

Ranger Four came back on the radio. "Send her to the banquet hall. I'll meet her there."

"Copy. Office One clear." When the mic locked back in its holster, she turned back to me. "See that building right across the way? Through those doors is the banquet hall. He'll be with you shortly."

"Thank you . . ?"

"Carmen. It's Carmen."

She held out her hand and shook mine as if she'd had one too many espressos that morning.

"It's nice to meet you."

"Likewise." She leaned in a bit closer. "You didn't hear it from me, but if he asks you your favorite kind of music, say Christmas."

I nodded. "Christmas music. Okay. Thanks."

"Anytime. I hope they keep ya."

I just smiled and turned to go, tugging my skirt down as I walked away. I hoped they kept me too.

The banquet hall was exactly as I'd expected: a large room with round tables and chairs dotting the hardwood floor. A door to my left likely led to a kitchen for caterers, and a small stage took up the far wall. The smell of freshly treated hardwood reminded me of the summer cabin my family had always rented.

I did my best to sit still and wait, but the waist of my pantyhose was starting to roll. I couldn't wait to be out of my interview attire and back into my yoga pants.

I heard his steps before I saw his face, boots on the wooden boardwalk leading up to the door. When he walked into the room, he flashed a big, genuine smile.

The light gray button-down shirt and navy cargo pants that made up his uniform only slightly diminished his hulking muscular form. Even though I was tall for a girl, I'd probably only come up to his armpit. A badge shone on his chest and a radio, pepper spray, multi-tool, flashlight, and an asp—a telescoping baton—hung from his belt.

"You must be Rylie."

I stood and shook his hand with the same firm grip my dad had shown me before my first job interview . . . as a babysitter.

"It's nice to meet you—uh—Ranger Four?"

"Ben." He chuckled.

"Ben." Big Ben. Easy to remember.

He motioned for me to sit before clicking the mic on his shoulder. "This is Ranger Four. I'll be off the radio for an interview. If you need me, call my cell."

"Copy," another male voice said. Ben snapped his radio off.

"Kyle—your direct supervisor—was supposed to be here for the interview, but he got held up in a meeting. So I'm afraid you're stuck with me." His grin was slightly apologetic. "In your application, I noticed you were a volunteer firefighter and have your degree"—his face lit up into a wide smile—"in Parks and Recreation Management from Denver State."

"That's correct." I returned the smile while trying to sit perched on the edge of the chair with my back as straight as possible.

"I went to Denver State too. Got the same degree. Don't let anyone tell you it's not a worthwhile one. It may not be wildlife management, but it's still been helpful to me all these years later."

"Good to know." It was always good to have something in common with the interviewer, right?

"Tell me about your time as a firefighter."

"I was with the Big Mountain Fire Department for about four years. Being a small town, we did more training than actual firefighting. Most of our job was assisting on medical calls and rescue situations, like ice rescue and vehicular accidents."

Ben pulled a notepad from his left breast pocket and jotted down a few notes as I spoke. His knuckles were covered in the same salt and pepper hair that made up the stubble on his face. "I can imagine those probably got pretty gruesome. Would you say you're well equipped to handle stressful situations?"

The time I'd been paged to a thirteen-car pile-up sprang to mind. Bodies lay strewn all over the ground, most of them dead. It had been me who rallied the other firefighters into action, set up triage. "I'd say I'm very well equipped."

Ben nodded knowingly. "And how do you feel those interactions would help you in your position as a park ranger?"

I thought about this for a minute. I likely wouldn't come across as many gruesome scenes as a park ranger. Images of fishermen with hooks in their hands came to mind. "I'm sure that as the first responders, rangers have to manage some of the same tasks I did when I was a fire-fighter. First aid, CPR, calling in additional help when needed. I'm trained in radio communication, and if I were able to stay on past the summer season, ice rescue." I sucked in a breath and tried to steady my nerves. When I got nervous, words spewed from my mouth. Verbal vomit, my ex used to call it. I hated that term . . . and him.

"And how about the law enforcement side of the job?"

My insides clenched. Other than working with law enforcement while I was a firefighter, and sleeping with a cop for the past five years, I had absolutely no experience in that realm. "As I understand it, the only law enforcement required would be to enforce park rules, which would be no problem."

"I see." He made another note.

If only I could have seen what he was writing. I knotted my hands in my lap. I needed this job. "If I'm wrong about the job description, let me know."

"No, that pretty much sums it up. We don't do a great deal of what you would think of as real law enforcement. Not exactly equipped, if you know what I mean?" He looked down at his belt where an asp rested in place of a gun.

Ben asked a few more questions. My strengths and weaknesses—attention to detail and organization. My likes and dislikes—Christmas music and spiders. Where I saw myself in five years—in a steady job and out of my parents' basement. Okay, so maybe I left out the part about my parents' basement.

"Well, it looks like everything is on the up and up. Can I answer any questions for you?"

I thought about it for a minute. "The job title is an urban park ranger. Does that mean I'll be required to go out into the city at times?"

"Good question. The answer is yes and no. As a summer ranger, you will primarily stay within the three city-owned reservoirs. There have been times, though, when summer rangers have gone on patrol on the trails that wind throughout the city. We are currently looking to obtain some additional land that butts up to the foothills and may even extend into the forest at some point, but that could be years away."

I nodded. "What does a typical schedule look like for a summer ranger?"

"You would work a week of morning shifts followed by a week of evening shifts. The reservoir hours change from month to month depending on sunrise and sunset, so your shifts will change to be earlier or later depending on opening and closing times. We also occasionally have overnight shifts when the reservoirs are closed, but we rarely require summer rangers to take those."

Overnight shifts with no one around and no gun to protect yourself? Sounded like a recipe for disaster to me.

"I think that's all the questions I have for now."

"Great." Ben stood and I followed suit. "Kyle said if everything seemed good that I should go forward with a job offer. Pending a background check, of course."

It took every bit of restraint in my body not to jump up and down with joy. I shook his hand. "Thank you so much."

As soon as Ben snapped his radio back on, chatter resumed.

"—white male running in the nude on the back side of the lake."

Ben let out a low groan. "I'd better go help. It was nice

to meet you, Rylie. I'll call you when the background check comes through and we can get you scheduled for training."

I nodded, but my mind had jumped from the interview to the call on his radio. Naked men? Better that than homeless drug dealers, murderers, and rabid dogs, I guessed.

———

Once back in the comfort of Cherry Anne, I shimmied out of the pantyhose and tossed them, along with the heels, into the back seat. When I looked up to start the engine, two men in gray and blue uniforms stood gaping at me.

Seriously? I know I looked around before removing the pantyhose. Maybe they didn't see anything?

Who was I kidding? By the look on their faces, they saw plenty.

The engine purred when I turned the key over, and I hit the button to roll down the window.

"Can I help you?" I asked in my most sincere and innocent voice.

They looked at each other like they'd forgotten what they were going to say. One was breathtakingly gorgeous, Italian, around thirty with muscles in all the right places. The other was tall and skinny with hints of gray peeking through his dark hair and a look on his face like he had a stick up his rear end.

"We certainly hope you can." The Italian one spoke first, his voice deep and warm like a vat of molten caramel. "Benny asked us to come up here and introduce ourselves."

"Don't you have a naked guy running through the park?"

He snickered. "Dusty and Seamus apprehended him." He offered his hand through the window. "My name is Antonio."

Of course it is.

"And I'm Kyle," the tall, skinny one said, "Your supervisor. I'm sorry I couldn't make it to the interview."

"It's no problem. Ben was very nice." I shook their hands in turn. "Pleasure to meet you both."

"The pleasure is all ours," Antonio said in his thick accent before Kyle elbowed him hard in the side.

"Ben said you'll be joining the team," Kyle said. "But I'd suggest you ditch the pantyhose."

"Done and done," I motioned to where I'd thrown them in the back of the car.

"Yes. We saw," Antonio said.

Kyle elbowed him even harder this time. "You can't talk to her like that. Remember the sexual harassment class we had to take?"

Antonio stuck out his chest. "They can't tame this Italian Stallion."

I stifled my giggle. Something about him was magnetic.

"Ranger Four, Ranger Two," Ben's voice crackled through their radios.

"Ranger Two," Kyle replied.

"If you and Ranger Six could come to the back of

Muddy Water Cove, it looks like the MWB has struck again."

"Copy, we'll be there shortly," Kyle said.

"Three clear."

"MWB?" I asked.

"Muddy Water Bandit. I came up with it," Antonio said through his devilishly handsome grin.

"It wasn't a hard name to come up with," Kyle said. "We have to go."

"Until we meet again." Antonio winked at me when Kyle wasn't looking.

They jumped into gigantic matching black Chevy pickup trucks and tore off in the direction opposite the exit.

Plopping my head back against the seat rest, I allowed a smile to breach my face. Finally, a job, no pantyhose required.

***

The drive back into the city from the reservoir took so long, I wondered if I had actually been in Wyoming. My parents made the idiotic decision to leave our beloved home in the mountains when I graduated high school, to move to this hellhole city filled with tree-huggers and their stupid sweater-wearing dogs. Who put a sweater on a dog anyway? They have this thing. It's called fur.

Pulling into their lower driveway, I dodged my sister's minivan and my brother-in-law's work truck. My parents parked in the attached garage, of course. Thankfully their house had been large enough for my sister, her husband,

and my four nephews to live in the apartment above the detached garage with their three ankle-biting dogs, while also allowing me to have their walkout basement all to myself.

It was bad enough I'd had to quit the fire department and flee my hometown when my ex and I split. But to my mother, boundaries were merely suggestions, especially when I was "living under her roof."

I tossed my keys onto one of the boxes stacked in the basement living room and shimmied off my skirt. While I was searching through my box of clothes for my favorite yoga pants, I heard my mother's voice behind me.

"How'd your interview go?"

"Mother!" I crouched trying to cover myself, knowing full well she had just gotten a great view of my bare ass.

"Oh, stop it." She didn't avert her eyes in the slightest. "I made you, birthed you, and bathed you. It's nothing I haven't seen before."

I grabbed the skirt and yanked it back on.

"So?"

"It went fine," I said in my most exasperated voice. "I got the job."

Her face didn't change. "You know, I worry this job will be too dangerous for you."

"I know, Mom. You told me this morning." I put my hands on my hips. "But it's no more dangerous than being a firefighter."

"*Volunteer* firefighter. It's not like you were in any real danger doing that."

I fought the urge to throw something at her. We had

been over the fact that the town only had volunteer fire-fighters, and we did everything paid firefighters did.

"Well, at least I got a job. A good job. A job that could turn into something more than just a job. Plus now I can save up and let you have your basement back."

"But you've only been here a week." Her lip jutted out in a pout. "And I like having the whole family back together. It feels right." She wrapped her arm around my shoulder and squeezed. "If it would make you feel better, I could start charging you rent."

I shook my head. "No. I don't want you to start charging me rent. This was supposed to be a way for me to get back on my feet after . . ."

She nodded slowly. "I told you that boy was trouble from the start. Kicking you out of his apartment for—what did you call her? Giraffe girl?" Every word was like salt in a wound. "Don't you like being here with us? Watching NASCAR and football games with your dad? Having family meals?"

This conversation was going to end up one of two ways: me hurting my mother's feelings by saying something stupid, or me lying and saving her feelings.

"Yes, Mom. It's nice to be home."

"Good." She squeezed me one last time and released me from her side hug. "Now come upstairs, I got Fizzy a present."

I looked around. Fizzy, my pit bull Lab mix, was surprisingly not weaving in and out of my legs like he usually did when I got home.

"What kind of present?" I asked, unsure I wanted the answer.

"Come upstairs and you'll see."

When I reached the top stair, the first thing I noticed was a look in my dog's eyes that I only ever saw when he was chasing cats. Murder. The second thing: a pink doggie sweater.

"Oh no. No, no, no." I walked over to where Fizzy sat next to my dad. "You cannot be serious."

"He was cold. I saw him shivering outside the other day and his hair is so short, so I bought him a sweater."

"Mom, it's almost summer. And he's . . . a boy."

"Boys can like pink. Your father has a pink tie."

My dad made a goofy face, and I tried not to laugh.

"Plus," she continued, "I am always shopping for my two-legged grandsons, but I never get to shop for my four-legged grandson."

"Please, do not tell me you just compared my sons—my human sons—to that mutt." My sister and her husband walked through the front door carrying two of their adorable and crazy little boys while the other two bounded in and knocked over a plant.

Megan, almost two years older than me, had her life together. She always looked like she had just emerged from the salon with her perfect brown ringlets. No one would guess she'd popped out four boys with her tiny frame. I had always been jealous of her petite stature, especially when she could wear the cute feminine clothes while I struggled to find ones that fit my taller and more muscular build.

"Oh, Megan, you know I love them all the same." My mom snatched up her oldest and planted a big kiss on his cheek—which he promptly wiped off.

"That's the problem." Megan shook her head. "They're humans." She pointed around to her boys. "And he's a dog." She pointed at a very anxious looking Fizzy. "*They* have your blood running through their veins. And *he* has cat guts rotting in his stomach."

"That's disgusting." Mom put the wiggling little boy back down. "And I won't have any talk like that under my roof."

"Sorry, Mom," Megan muttered before turning her attention to me. "Ry, did you get the job?"

I nodded. "Sixth time's the charm."

"But she's not sure if she's going to take it yet," Mom said.

"Um, I already accepted the position." Not quite true, but I had every intention to when my background check cleared.

"Why wouldn't she take the position?" My brother-in-law, Tom, sat down on the couch next to Megan.

"It's just so dangerous. There are all those criminals and—"

"She'll be fine," my father piped in. "She's a smart girl. She can handle herself."

"Thanks, Daddy." I planted a kiss on his cheek. "Now, let's get this thing off Fizzy."

2

———

I f my first shift was any indicator, being a ranger was going to be nothing like I expected.

"Let me show you around," Ben said when I arrived at the massive shop on a hill overlooking Alder Ridge Reservoir. "This is where we are stationed. From the outside it doesn't look like much, but inside it's our haven."

He was right. Outside it looked like any other metal post frame building with five huge garage doors and a single man door. No windows. But once you were inside, it was as if I'd stepped into the ultimate man cave. The garage area had enough space to house five large ranger trucks and two smaller ones, two boats—though only one was actually on its trailer, and a wash bay that was completely decked out.

"How else do you think we'd keep the trucks clean?" Ben shrugged. "And then in here, we have our offices."

He opened a door that led to several cubicles and a

large round table with chairs surrounding it. The smell of cologne and Doritos hit my nose, reminding me of the firehouse.

"But the best part is in the loft . . ." he looked up.

My gaze followed his to where a metal railing cordoned off a large section above the offices. When we got to the top of the spiral staircase, the expanse opened up into a recreational area. There was a pool table, workout equipment, a worn leather sofa, a large flat screen TV, and two cots with a white blanket and pillow folded nicely at the foot. And a small kitchenette sported a mini fridge.

"They made this because they thought it'd make us hang out here during our time off. Make us more available if something happened and the rangers on duty needed backup."

"And did you?"

"Not really. I mean, sometimes we do, but it's not like we can enjoy a beer and watch the game. Alcohol is expressly forbidden. Plus there's cameras." He pointed to a far corner. "Why would we want to hang out when Big Brother's watching?"

He had a point. What a waste of space.

"And over here we have the locker rooms, storage closets, and training rooms. This is where you'll go through your summer ranger training."

I nodded and tried to take it all in. The space was well designed. It almost felt like a hip club, without the alcohol, of course.

"I set aside a uniform for you," He pointed to one of the chairs in the training room where a pile of clothes lay unfolded. "Go in and try it on. It probably won't be perfect, but summies don't get much other option."

"Summies?" I quirked an eyebrow at him.

He let out a booming laugh. "Summer rangers. We call them summies."

Muddy Water Bandit? Summies? They needed serious help coming up with nicknames.

Not only was the uniform not perfect, it was practically unwearable. The pants were at least two sizes too big and the shirt had stains that could rival those of my Uncle Jeff's—an over-the-road truck driver with a hole in his lip. Thankfully, the belt had already been outfitted with various holsters, and it cinched tight enough to keep my pants from settling in around my ankles.

"Not too shabby," Ben said when I emerged from the bathroom. "But where's the hat?"

I pulled out the most disgusting hat I'd ever seen. "It smells like someone died in it."

"Nah, no one's died here in years." Ben chuckled. "A quick run through the dishwasher, and it'll be good as new."

I seriously doubted my mother was going to let such filth anywhere near her dishwasher, let alone in her house. I pulled my long, freshly highlighted blonde hair into a ponytail and out the back of the hat, promising myself I'd shower and run the hat through a gallon of bleach when I got home.

Ben's black Chevy let out a low rumble when he turned the key, and Christmas music blared from its Bose speakers. Interesting use of taxpayer money, but hey, I didn't live in this city.

"Sorry about that. I'm a Christmas-all-the-time kind of guy. That's part of the reason I hired you." He turned the radio down.

Only part of me felt bad that I'd exaggerated my love of Christmas music. At least it had gotten me the job. I made a mental note to thank Carmen.

"Now, normally we don't ride together. It's a waste of resources to have us both in one truck. But since I'm training you, the rules are different. When we're out on patrol, we're not only looking for people doing something wrong. We also answer questions, help out, and even make small talk. Fishermen love to talk. Especially with the female rangers."

I bet they did.

We began our daily route from the large shop where the ranger trucks were parked at night when the park was closed. The lake, a striking shade of blue, reflected the nearly cloudless sky. Sailboats and kayaks floated along lazily while fishermen dotted the shorelines.

"You met Antonio and Kyle, right?" He grinned but didn't take his eyes off the road.

"Yeah, they're—"

"Quite the pair."

"Oh, they're . . . together?" How had I missed that?

Ben inhaled sharply and began choking on his spit. "If they heard you thought—" He tried to keep talking but his face was turning red from laughter and a lack of oxygen. "No. *No.*" He shook his head and veered the truck to one side allowing a bike to pass. "They're just friends." He finally regained part of his composure. "They're both married. To women."

"Married?" I didn't know what was more disappointing, the thought of Antonio being gay or married.

Ben quirked an eyebrow at me. "Antonio gave you the goo-goo eyes, didn't he?" He shook his head. "That's just like him. Always flirting with the summies."

Heat rose in my cheeks. It wasn't as if I was looking for a relationship at this point anyway. But knowing I was just one in a handful of flirtations stung.

"If I could give you one bit of advice, it would be to stay away from him. He's nothing but trouble. It's a wonder his wife puts up with his antics."

"Noted." I plastered on a smile and changed the subject. "I heard over the radio the other day that you're dealing with a Muddy Water Bandit?"

"Yep." Ben took a turn around a corner and a row of gigantic houses appeared beyond the park fence line. "Someone has been trapping catfish—or at least trying to —in the back of Muddy Water Cove. We've removed several traps, but it hasn't stopped. This lake is home to some of the biggest catfish in the state."

"Yeah, I read about the state record in the paper. I guess I never knew Colorado had catfish, let alone ones as big as the record breaker."

Ben pulled off to the side of the trail and shut the engine off. "Good ol' Ronnie. He's quite the character. Just wait until you meet him." He motioned for me to get out of the truck.

I jumped down and pulled up my pants, making a mental note to wear briefs rather than a thong my next shift. At least then if my pants fell, the fishermen wouldn't get an eyeful.

"We'll go down and make conversation, check licenses, and then move on. These are the interactions that make up at least seventy-five percent of our job."

I trudged through the brush and tried to keep up with Ben's long steps. My brand new work boots were already hurting my feet. As we approached, the smell of something rotting made my insides heave. It was even worse than the stench wafting from my hat.

"Hey, Dave," Ben said. The fisherman I'd seen in the office before my interview stood with his back to us. "How's the fishing?"

"It's shit," he said without turning around. He held out a blue piece of paper, folded several times to be the size of a driver's license. Ben took it from him and looked it over. "How many times have you checked my license this week?" He glared at Ben with contempt.

"You know I have to check everyone. If I skip you, the next person will ask why I didn't check yours."

"There ain't nobody else out here." Dave scanned the area until his eyes came to rest on me. He looked me up and down before letting out a low whistle. "You sure know how to pick the pretty ones, Benny." He winked at Ben and grinned at me, demonstrating the side effects of chewing tobacco.

"Don't give her a hard time," Ben said. "She'll be with us for the summer."

"Someday you're gonna have to keep one of them."

I tried my best not to grimace at the way his eyes lingered on my chest while he ran his tongue between his rotted front teeth.

"It's gotta be boring working with the same six dudes for the past ten years."

Ben shrugged.

"I'm sure you've seen a Colorado fishing license before." He handed me the long, unfolded piece of glossy blue paper. "But you've probably never inspected one as closely as we do when we do our checks. The biggest thing is to make sure it's the proper year and that the physical description matches the person who gave it to us. We can always ask for a driver's license to verify their identity if we need to."

"You guys take this fishing business way too seriously," Dave said.

"*We* do?" Ben handed him the license back. "As I hear it, you were giving Carmen quite the earful about your suspicions the other day."

Dave's eyes narrowed. "He's cheating, Benny. We all know he didn't catch that fish legally."

"We found nothing to suggest Ronnie caught the fish *illegally*." Ben lifted his hat from his forehead and scratched at his receding hairline.

"What about those traps back in Muddy Cove? Those ain't suspicious to you?" Dave cast his lure back into the water.

"And how exactly do you know about the traps?" Ben's tone was still jovial, but his eyes focused in on Dave as if searching for a sign of guilt.

"You know how it goes. No one can keep a secret around here."

Ben didn't immediately respond.

I looked back and forth between the two men. Just as

the silence was becoming awkward, Ben took a step toward Dave, his voice so quiet I could barely hear, "What secrets do you keep?"

Dave turned to look Ben in the eye. "Wouldn't you like to know?" Dave muttered. "All I'll say is if I knew for certain Ronnie caught that state record catfish using an illegal trap, he'd be in a world of hurt."

Ben let out a sigh. "Have a nice day, Dave."

Once we were back at the truck, I let out a small laugh. "He's intense."

"You'll get used to him, and all the others. Fishermen are a different bunch, a lot of them don't have much of a filter."

Probably not that different from some of the cretins I encountered as a firefighter. It could be downright infuriating having to put up with their crap, but biting my tongue was the professional thing to do.

"So, that's the basics of what we do. We check licenses. If someone is fishing without a license we can give them a ticket or a warning—but we'll get into that in training."

"I hate to ask, but what was that awful smell? Does Dave have something against personal hygiene?"

Ben let out a laugh so loud, I thought Dave might hear. "No, no. That's catfish bait. They call it stink bait, for obvious reasons. Catfish love it—can't get enough."

I wrinkled my nose. Why a fish would want to eat something that smelled worse than a rotting corpse was beyond me.

"But I wouldn't be surprised if Dave hadn't showered

in several days either." He laughed again. "You're going to fit right in."

He put the truck in gear.

"How about we go back and check Muddy Water Cove for traps?" He aimed the truck down a dirt path.

"From what Dave said back there, it sounds like there's not much room for advancement." I kept my eyes trained on the path ahead of us.

"Oh, yeah," Ben said. "I hope that doesn't mean you'll be leaving us."

Did it? "Nah, I need the job, even if it is only for the summer." Maybe I could save enough to get a tiny apartment. In the slums.

"Great." Ben let out a breath. "Looks like we might have some action in the cove." He turned toward a beautiful, tree-lined bit of water that branched off the main reservoir. The depths were deep blue and anything but muddy.

"Why do you call it Muddy Water Cove?"

"Because that's its name." He smiled at me and then turned off the ignition.

How had Ben noticed any activity in the cove? Not a single person was in this part of the park, and—as far as I could tell—not one visible sign of a trap.

"Right here," he said when we reached the shoreline. "See those swirls on the surface?" He plunged his massive arms into the water and pulled hard on a line of green and purple rope. His tanned muscles tensed and his veins popped as he tugged one hand over another. But aside from an intensely concentrated stare and a tiny bead of sweat on his forehead, Ben made the task look as easy as reeling in an empty fishing line. Finally, an enormous metal contraption broke the surface of the glassy water. Nothing but reeds and bits of mud stuck to the bottom of the cage.

"This is the seventh one we've confiscated." He walked the trap up to the truck and threw it into the bed without so much as a grunt. "You'd think this guy—or girl, I suppose"—he made a motion toward me as if trying to be politically correct—"would be tired of spending the money and go back to using a line and pole."

"Have you ever confiscated one with an actual catfish in it?"

"Nope. Not one."

Wow. This guy was an idiot. Like one of my college professors used to say, "The definition of stupidity is doing the same thing twice and expecting different results." I was pretty sure Einstein said that was the definition of insanity—either way, if the shoe fit . . .

Muddy Water Cove seemed to go on forever as we drove around several twists and turns, the water still shimmering from behind trees and bushes to our left.

"You'll notice five walk-in gates along the fence line where visitors can park their cars in the neighborhoods and walk into the reservoir." Ben pointed up a dirt path leading to an open gate. "Every morning we open them and every evening we close them. It can be tedious, but if you're late, you'll get an earful from the fishermen. Sometimes they'll even call the City Offices and then things get really sticky, so don't dawdle in the mornings."

"Gotcha." I made a mental note to always get to the gates on time.

"There are three coves at Alder Ridge Reservoir. The one closest to the plaza and beach area is called Marina Cove because people pay to leave their boats attached to buoys for the summer. Muddy Water Cove is different from the others because it has trees and bushes lining the shore."

He pointed to the natural landscaping.

"And then there's Long Beach Cove where there's—"

"Let me guess, no beach?" I laughed at my own joke.

Ben looked confused. "No, there's a beach. All along the shoreline."

Of course there was. "I just thought because Muddy Water Cove wasn't really muddy . . . "

"Oh, I see!" Ben let out a laugh. "That is funny."

When we finally reached what had to be the opposite side of the cove—though the shoreline where we'd confiscated the trap was completely hidden from view—we stopped again to talk to a fisherman.

"Hey, Jackson," Ben said. The man was Dave's complete opposite. He was tall and dark with broad shoulders and a handsomely groomed beard. Where Dave looked to be around forty-five, Jackson was a solid twenty-two. The fishing gear around him was neatly organized into straight rows, from small to large, and color-coded.

"Ben," he said with a charming smile. "And this is—?"

"Rylie," I replied.

"Nice to meet you, Rylie."

"Likewise," I said.

"Jackson used to be one of our summies but has since moved on to be a state park ranger."

"The fishing is still better here, though," Jackson said handing Ben his fishing license.

"Hey, how long have you been here?" Ben asked. "We just found another trap on the far side of the cove."

"Not long," Jackson threw out his line with grace and accuracy that could only have come from years of practice. "I thought I would come out for a bit while the husband is shopping."

"Any luck?"

"Nothing. Not a single bite," Jackson slowly reeled in his line, tugging up then reeling in the slack over and over again to make his lure dance beneath the water's surface. I watched, mesmerized by the smooth pull and quick flick of his wrist. He was good. "I don't see how Ronnie did it."

"Dave thinks Ronnie is the MWB and that's how he caught the fish," Ben said.

Jackson's jaw tensed a bit. "I don't know if I would be pissed or relieved to find out he caught that cat with a trap."

"I'll let you get back to it." Ben handed his license back. "Tell Craig I say hi."

"Will do."

I'd never fished like Jackson before. Not only were my movements jerky and haphazard, typically all my crap was spread out randomly, and I used worms and marshmallow-esque bait. Maybe that's why I never caught anything, not that Jackson was catching anything with his fancy moves.

"Nice meeting you, Rylie. I'm sure I'll see you around." He put a hand up to the side of his mouth as if telling me a secret. "Don't let this guy bore you with his endless stories."

I laughed and nodded.

Ben rolled his eyes and motioned toward the truck.

The truck doors were so far from the ground I was certain my ass would be three inches higher by the time the summer was over from all the getting in and out. At least it meant I didn't need to do so many squats.

"Do all the rangers fish?" I asked as we headed back to the main plaza area.

"For the most part," Ben said. "Some of us are more, um, meticulous and enthusiastic than others."

I chuckled. "Like Jackson?"

"Yeah, and Antonio and Kyle are known to fish quite a bit too. It's easy to become obsessed. Fishing can be as addicting as smoking or drugs. Some of these guys have failed marriages and estranged children because they can't kick the just-one-more-fish mentality."

"And you? Do you fish?"

"Not as much as I used to. My wife and kids are my world. I have two teenage sons"—he pulled down his sun visor where a picture of his family was taped up—"and a ten-year-old daughter. They're my life. Fishing, well, let's just say talking about it all day five days a week is enough for me."

I smiled.

"How about you?" he asked.

"Do I fish or do I have a family?"

"Either, both?"

"I've fished since I was a little girl. My dad took me out all the time, but my favorite was ice fishing. Probably

28

the snowmobile part, more than the fishing part though." I smiled to myself. I hadn't thought of those memories for a long time. "And I don't have a family of my own, not yet anyway. I just got out of a relationship . . ."

"Sorry, I didn't mean to pry—"

"Oh, no, don't worry about it," I said more happily than I intended. "It was for the best. You'd think I'd have learned after five years, but I guess I'm a bit stubborn."

"Women always think they can change a man. Doesn't work."

Didn't I know it? I sighed.

Ben rounded a corner and the thatched roofs of the plaza buildings came into view. The swim beach was clean, its golden sand completely empty of visitors. Marina Cove held five sailboats and two fishing boats that moved in a synchronized dance with the waves. It was so peaceful and breathtaking.

"Looks like you'll get to meet our local celebrity," he said, pulling into a parking lot filled with trucks and small boat trailers.

As we approached a rusted-out Ford Ranger, the man whose face I had seen on the cover of the newspaper waved. Ben parked next to the truck and rolled down his window.

"How's it going, Benny?" Ronnie Tilsdale shoved his hands into his back pockets and rocked back on his heels. He was even smaller than he looked in the newspaper photo.

"It's a beautiful day to catch some fish."

"Have you been back in the cove? Anyone catching

anything back there?" Ronnie's beady eyes darted to the back of the pickup where the trap lay in plain sight.

"Not that I've heard. Looks like you caught the only cat in that cove." Ben leaned back in his seat so Ronnie could see me. "This is our newest ranger. Rylie."

I smiled and raised my hand in a short wave. "Nice to meet you, Ronnie. I saw you in the paper."

His face brightened with a huge smile. "Thankfully, they got my good side."

"They sure did," I said as seriously as I could. Both of his "sides" looked the same to me.

"I see you pulled up another trap." Ronnie's smile faded slightly. "You know the rumors ain't true, right, Benny? I didn't catch that fish with nothing but a line and pole."

He looked like he was telling the truth. Plus, there was no way this tiny mouse of a man would have been able to throw that trap into the water, let alone get it all the way out there by himself.

"Do you know who might have put out the traps?" Ben asked. "You're here so often, I'd be surprised if you haven't unknowingly seen them."

Ronnie ran a hand through his greasy black hair. "I don't wanna make no accusations. It wouldn't be—"

"I'm not asking you to accuse anyone," Ben said.

Ronnie rocked back on his heels. "The only people I seen fishing back there with any regularity are your ranger buddies, Ding Dong Dave, and my old pal Clark—but he ain't been around since I caught the record. We got in a argument, and he decided to take his fishing elsewhere."

"Well, if you see anything else, let me know," Ben said. "Good luck out there today."

"Thanks. It was nice meetin' ya, Rylie. I'll be seeing you more this summer, I hope." And he winked at me. Ugh.

Before Ben had time to roll up his window and put the truck in gear, the door to Ronnie's truck swung open and an Amazonian woman emerged, yelling at the top of her lungs. "Flirting with the rangers now? She ain't gonna give you a second look, you worm." Ronnie cowered beneath her presence. "Ain't no husband of mine gonna look at no other woman."

"I—I'm sorry, darlin'."

"Don't you darlin' me. You's about the dumbest man on the face of this world. Didn' I tell ya last time, the next time you looked at another woman, there'd be consequences?"

She raised her fist, and Ronnie covered his face with his hands.

"Ma'am, I'm going to need you to calm down." Ben opened the door and stepped out, his height matching hers. I followed suit and hurried around the truck to stand next to Ben.

Ronnie's wife dropped her arm as if she'd forgotten we were there in the first place.

"It's okay," Ronnie said. "She's right. I shouldn'ta been flirtin' with the pretty—I mean, not pretty. She's not pretty, she's hideous—"

Hideous?

Her eyes darted between Ben and me before she

turned to Ronnie and barked out, "Get in the truck. No fishin' for you today."

Ronnie looked defeated. "Sorry you had to see that, Benny. She's not usually like this. She ain't been the same since Clark disappeared." He looked at me, shoulders slumped, and tightened his mouth—as if he'd wanted to say something. Then, he climbed into the truck.

Ben chuckled and shook his head. "And I bet you thought this job was going to be boring."

I don't know what I thought, but this definitely wasn't it. I mean, where were the naked men?

"We should probably head up to the shop before Antonio and Kyle leave for the day."

My heart fluttered in my chest.

No. He was married.

One of the large garage doors to the shop was open and Kyle and Antonio stood chatting by their trucks.

"Hey Rylie," Antonio said as we approached. "How's your first day been?"

"Good so far." I shrugged and tried not to blush.

"She met Jackson and Dave and Ronnie," Ben said.

"Fishin' in the cove?" Kyle asked, his face perking up.

"Jackson and Dave were. Ronnie had to go home. His wife put her foot down."

"She's terrifying," Antonio said. "Like a bear."

"Were Jackson and Dave catching anything?" Kyle asked, clearly not caring how terrifying Ronnie's wife was.

"Nah, but there was another trap," Ben said walking back to his truck. We all followed.

"Another one? Wow, this guy's determined," Antonio said.

"We took the others over to the storage block at Shadow Trail. I can take this one with me and drop it off on my way home." Kyle lifted the trap into the back of his personal pickup truck. "That had to be how Ronnie caught that cat. He and Clark were all up in arms with each other when they came in to report the catch. Definitely something going on there. There's no way Ronnie'd catch that cat before me or Antonio or Jackson. Hell, even Dave's a better fisherman than Ronnie."

Kyle's face was turning red. Part of me wanted to pat him on the back and tell him it would be okay, like I did when my nephews fought over their toys.

"It's all right buddy, we'll get ours." Antonio slapped Kyle on the back. "But tonight we have an Avs game to watch. Benny, you comin' over after you close?"

"Your parties are a bit too much for me. Last time I had a hangover for a week." Ben absentmindedly rubbed his head. "I'll pass."

"Well, I'll be there," Kyle said. "Just as soon as I get this trap over to Shadow Trail and throw the pole in a few times." He turned his attention to me. "Is Ben doing a good job training you?"

"So far, so good." I shot Ben a sideways grin.

"Good." Kyle's sharp tone and raised eyebrow caught me off guard. "Remember, you'll be tested on what you learn about the reservoir. It's not just a social hour."

I nodded, unsure how to respond.

Antonio and Kyle both got into their personal vehicles —an old red Ford pickup for Kyle and a decked out black Cadillac CTS-V for Antonio—and tore off like teenagers spinning out on the gravel.

Ben shook his head. "Some boys never grow up."

The rest of the shift was full of Ben's stories. Jackson wasn't lying. He had more stories than I could have ever remembered. Admittedly some weren't so bad. Like the one about the biker who peed on a "No Motorcycle Parking" sign after being ticketed for parking in front of it.

Closing down the reservoir for the night started with locking all the plaza buildings including the main office, the banquet hall, and the multiple bathroom structures that lined the boardwalk between the beach and the picnic areas. The trees cast eerie shadows across the grass making me more jumpy than usual. Hopefully, I'd get used to all the sights and sounds before I had to do this on my own.

Once the plaza area was locked up, we moved on to closing the gates and checking one last time to see if the Muddy Water Bandit had placed another trap. Two in one day? I didn't think it was likely, but I went along with Ben's plan even though my eyelids were heavy and my feet blistered.

At the cove, something was off. The water certainly swirled like Ben had mentioned before, but in the fading sunlight, I couldn't make out what made the water churn.

"Looks like a trap may have finally caught something

after all," Ben said. "I just hope it's alive and we can release it."

The thought of touching one of those massive mucous-covered fish with tentacle whiskers made me cringe. Hopefully, the trap had captured a bass or a trout or something like the fish I used to catch in the mountains.

Ben's arms strained as he pulled the rope. Even with his bulky muscles, he struggled against the weight. I got behind him and helped pull. Hand over hand, the line taut with deadweight. By the time we got the trap onto the bank—a full fifteen minutes later—we both reeked of sweat. I was covered in it, my skin cooling too quickly in the chilly evening. My arms shook with fatigue.

The last light of sun had faded, and darkness overtook the cove.

Ben pulled his flashlight from his belt and shone it at the cage. The light found—not a fish—but rather what looked like a boot, then a torso, and finally came to rest on a blotchy and bloated face.

Death was unmistakable.

It didn't matter how many I'd come across as a firefighter, dead bodies were never easy to see.

Instead of panic, my mind flew into problem-solving mode. Ben's eyes widened as he lunged toward where a boot protruded from one end of the cage.

"We can't disturb the crime scene," I put a hand out to stop him. "Don't touch the body."

"But what if we can—maybe we can do something . . ."

I pulled on a pair of gloves and placed two fingers through the cage, to the side of the slimy neck knowing full well I wouldn't find a pulse. "There's nothing we can do. He's gone."

Ben stood like a statue. His flashlight still focused on the man's face. "Ronnie," he mumbled. "I can't believe . . ."

I hadn't made the connection until he said the name. It was most definitely Ronnie.

"You need to radio the police," I choked back the tears in my throat, took a deep breath, and regained my composure. I know I had only met him that day, but seeing someone dead who had been alive mere hours before was surreal.

Ben robotically turned the dials and found the appropriate channel before calling out on his radio, "We have a Code Fifty-Five at Alder Ridge Reservoir in the back of Muddy Water Cove."

The dispatcher promised to send officers straight away.

"Sometimes they don't know where they're going," Ben's normal jovial voice was now monotone. "We've tried to work with them, but they think we're a joke."

His rambling continued for what seemed like an hour before the lights of a police car peeked over the ridge. Two officers stepped out with their flashlights pointed at us.

"We hear you got a body on your hands." The first one, a short stalky man with a handlebar mustache, smiled as if discussing the latest town gossip, his voice a mix of a bullfrog and a growling dog.

The second man was about twice his partner's height, with arms the size of beach balls, and a face that was vaguely—

"Rylie?"

Even after ten years, there was no mistaking that voice.

"Luke?" I raised my hand in a stunned wave. Luke had been my first real boyfriend. My first kiss. My first, well, everything. And I hadn't seen him in years.

"Looks like this guy's got himself into a bit of trouble." Luke's partner pulled on a pair of gloves and walked gingerly around the scene.

"What are you doing here? Dressed like . . . that?"

He was dressed differently too. His usual preppy attire was replaced with a uniform and gun. His aviator glasses perched gently in his perfectly gelled brown hair.

"I'm a park ranger—a summer park ranger." I squared my shoulders, thankful he couldn't see how disgusting my uniform was in the darkness.

"A park ranger? What happened to firefighting?" His face had always given away his emotions, but in the dark I couldn't make out what he was thinking. He knew my ex. We'd all grown up together. Surely he'd heard the gossip. Heck, he may have known about the indiscretions before I had.

"It's a long story."

"We don't have time for long stories." Luke's partner interrupted. "We need to get the coroner and the forensic team out here. Looks like it's going to be a long night for all of us."

A long night was an understatement. Ben and I had to finish locking up the park and lead the coroner and the forensic team to the body. Then we waited, and waited, and waited.

Once Ben snapped out of his stupefied daze, he explained how we couldn't leave when there were others in the park, even other law enforcement. I spent most of the night sitting in the truck answering questions like "When did you find the body?" and "Are you certain of the identity?"

Occasionally, Luke tried to sneak away to chat, but his partner wasn't about to let him slack off and catch up with me. Which was okay since I wasn't exactly on my A game.

Finally, the sun came up. Antonio and Kyle were there for their opening shift, both looking like they'd had a long night of drinking. I was so exhausted by the time I got home I nearly fell asleep standing in the shower.

My mother chewed me up one side and down the other about how she was so worried when they saw footage of the scene from an air traffic helicopter on the early news. I almost reminded her that I was supposed to be given all the freedoms of living on my own, even though I was in her basement, but I didn't have the energy. I only had a few hours to sleep before I had to report back for training, and hopefully, a less eventful shift.

3

I awoke to the sound of my phone's alarm blaring in my ear. I must have fallen asleep perusing social media. My job status needed updating, but if I didn't get my butt in gear and to work, it would stay at "unemployed."

It seemed like I had only just been there—probably because I had—and the thought of going through a shift with any sense of normalcy was a stretch. Not that I really knew what normal looked like.

Ben met me in the shop's wash bay, where most of the rangers probably spent a great deal of time washing their prized trucks—not unlike we had at the fire department. Ben was diligently drying the passenger door of his pickup when I walked in.

"Any word?" I asked.

He wrung out the chamois and kept drying without meeting my gaze. "Preliminary investigation says he got caught in his own trap and drowned."

39

"They think Ronnie was the MWB?"

"They couldn't find any other cause of death, but they're doing an autopsy, so maybe we'll hear more later." The cheerfulness hadn't returned to his voice. Instead he sounded empty, hollow.

I knew the feeling. The first time I saw a dead person, I wasn't right for a month. Granted it had been a much more gruesome scene, but still, death wasn't easy, especially when you knew the deceased.

"I'm sorry, Ben," I said.

He looked up at me and half-smiled. "Don't be sorry, I'm okay. Are you feeling up to training today? The other summies will be here any minute, but if you're tired and want to go home—"

"Nah, I slept plenty. Bring on the training," I said with as much enthusiasm as I could muster. The gigantic latte I'd gulped down on my way to work should be enough to sustain me through the first half of the shift.

"I'll walk with you upstairs." He wrung out the chamois one last time and hung it on a rack to dry.

"Are you instructing the training today?"

"No, I'll be on patrol." He rubbed his temples. "Greg, Ranger One, will be starting off."

Greg looked too kind to be a Ranger. His salt and pepper hair, mixed with his thick-framed glasses and genuine grin, made him more akin to a lovable grandfather than an enforcer. Two other summer rangers sat side by side at a long table facing the front where Greg stood. I was the last to arrive and sat at the very end, closest to the door.

First order of business was to go down the table and introduce ourselves.

The girl next to me began. She was in her early twenties, a bit hefty, and looked uncomfortable sitting in the middle of the room with all attention on her. Her curly blonde hair was pulled back into a ponytail, and she wore more makeup than was necessary, but it worked for her.

"My name is Shayla," she said just above a whisper, her cheeks flushing a deep crimson. "I want to go into law enforcement like my mother, and I thought this would be a good place to start. I obviously am not going to be running any marathons this summer," she giggled and patted her belly, "but I hope to utilize this position to get into better shape so I can try out for the police academy in the fall."

"I'm Brock," the man on the other side of Shayla said. I cringed. Putting way too much effort into sounding manly, Brock was a skinny five-foot-seven with sandy blond hair and testosterone surging out of every pore on his body. His cologne was too strong, his hair too gelled. "I wanted to be a State Park Ranger, but they told me to start here."

Probably because they didn't want you around them. I imagined him standing next to Jackson and almost let out a laugh.

"I'm newly married." He held up his left ring finger and waved it around so Shayla and I could see. How were all of these twenty-year-olds getting married when I was getting closer and closer to thirty every day without so much as a proposal?

"Congratulations, Brock," Greg said with a smile. To which Brock nodded.

"I'm Rylie," I said, my pulse quickening. I hated public speaking. "I have a degree in Parks and Recreation Management, and between that and my background in firefighting it seemed to fit. So, here I am."

"Rylie's background check came through early, so she has actually been here an extra day. You had quite the shift yesterday, didn't you?" Greg said.

"I did." If only my background check had come through at normal speed. "Ben—uh, Ranger Four—and I came across a dead body stuck in a trap in the back of Muddy Water Cove."

Shayla gasped and clapped a hand over her mouth, her eyes gigantic like those stuffed animals you'd find in a resort gift shop.

"Traps are illegal, per rule…" Brock pulled out a copy of the park rules and regulations from a large folder of information he had apparently studied prior to training.

"Yeah," I continued while he paged through the regulation book, "It appears Ronnie Tilsdale was the victim of his own trap. They're calling him the Muddy Water Bandit. But that's just preliminary—"

"And none of that leaves this room," Greg said.

"But my wife and I tell each other everything." Brock snapped the regulation book closed.

Greg shook his head. "Confidentiality is king—or er, queen too." He looked at Shayla and me apologetically. "It's an ongoing investigation, meaning you must not speak to anyone about the details of this case or any sensitive information you may learn on the job, really."

After he pulled down a projector screen, Greg dimmed the lights. "But to get back on topic, it's very nice to meet all of you. As you know, I'm Greg—Ranger One—but I'm only number one because I've been here since the beginning of the program nearly forty years ago. It has its benefits since I'm technically in charge. But don't think of me as your boss. Kyle is really your direct supervisor as he's in charge of the summer ranger program." He pushed a button on a remote and a picture of a smaller reservoir popped up. "This is where it all started—Shadow Trail Reservoir." He flipped to a more recent picture. "As you can see, it's grown quite a bit in the last twenty years."

The picture did show growth, more around the edges of the reservoir than the actual reservoir itself. Where there had been fields and trees surrounding the pristine water, houses were now stacked closely all the way up to the fence that separated them from the reservoir.

"We've grown from a staff of one"—he pulled up a picture of himself no older than twenty-five with the same goofy grin and warmth behind his eyes—"to a staff of six." Six semi-smiling faces stared at us. I recognized four of them now. The other two I still hadn't met.

Greg continued on for about three hours going over every detail of the history. The promised buzz of my coffee exited the building at hour two, leaving me struggling to keep my eyes open.

"Let's break for fifteen minutes," Greg said.

We let out a unanimous sigh of relief.

"What did he look like?" Shayla turned to me with the same gigantic and completely endearing eyes. "Ronnie. I mean, I've never seen a dead guy before."

"Cold, blue, stuck in a catfish cage," I said as evenly as possible.

Shayla stuck out her tongue. "I didn't know catfish cages were that big."

I shook my head. "They're not, but neither was Ronnie."

"You must have seen a lot of shit as a firefighter," Brock said. "I wanted to be a firefighter once, but I wanted to have a gun more."

Something inside me was thankful he didn't actually have a gun. He seemed like the type to accidentally shoot off his own toe while trying to spin it around his finger in front of the bathroom mirror.

"Do state park rangers have guns?" I asked.

"Yep, they're technically certified the same as the police," Brock said. "They even go through the same police academy."

Shayla nodded. "I thought about starting with state parks, but their rangers are just so high strung. These guys are way nicer." She motioned around at Greg who was humming a tune to himself with a smile on his face.

Maybe they were a bit too nice.

"Have you met the other rangers?" Shayla asked.

"Not all of them," I replied. "I've met Kyle—Ranger Two, Ben—Four, and Antonio—Six."

"What are they like? Well, other than Kyle." She looked over at Brock. "We met him in the interview."

"Ben is great. Super smart and has a lot of stories. A big family man. And Antonio—" I searched for the right words. Hot and flirtatious didn't seem appropriate for small talk. "Antonio's a character."

"Well, hello, Ben." Greg slapped Ben on the back.

Ben half-smiled and then looked at me. "I need to borrow you for a second."

"Oh sure, go ahead, go ahead," Greg said. "We'll be here when you get back."

Part of me was thrilled that Ben had saved me from the droning history lesson, but the other part was worried that something was wrong. Had I already made a mistake? Was it about Ronnie?

"Officer Hannah is here to discuss some new details in the drowning case." Ben led me to the banquet hall.

Luke sat at one of the tables looking far too relaxed—and sexy. Flashbacks of all the times his arms had wrapped around my waist from behind sent shivers down my spine. A feeling of suffocation quickly followed. Surely he wasn't the same person as he was in high school, he'd probably learned by now to give his girlfriend breathing room. Though I didn't know if I even deserved another chance with him after everything that happened with us. Everything I'd done wrong.

His easy grin broke into a wide smile when our eyes met, and I locked my knees so they wouldn't betray me and leave me lying in a heap on the floor. Had he always been that good-looking?

"Hey, Ry," he said.

"Hi, Luke."

Ben cleared his throat, breaking our connection, allowing me to take a breath.

"You have some updates for us?" Ben asked as we sat.

"Yeah, looks like it wasn't an accidental drowning after all." Luke exchanged his smile for a concentrated frown.

He looked down at his cell phone and continued. "From the medical examiner's notes, looks like Tilsdale's cause of death was strangulation by the same purple and green rope found attached to the catfish cage. His lungs contained no water. He was dead before submersion."

"So this was murder," I said more to myself than anyone else. "But how did we miss the strangulation marks? I checked for a pulse and didn't feel or see anything."

Ben's face drained of color.

"To be fair, it was dark and he was in a cage and slimy. We didn't catch it either." Luke tucked his phone back into the pocket of his shirt. "And since this is now a murder investigation, I'll need to ask you a few more questions."

When Ben didn't speak up, I said, "Of course, whatever we can do to help."

"I need to interview each ranger working the day you found the body."

"Kyle and Antonio opened, and Rylie and I closed," Ben replied. "You don't think one of us . . ." Ben started but seemed to choke on the words.

"I don't think anything right now," Luke said. "I'm only here to do my job."

"I'll start," I said. "Where do you want to do this interview?"

Luke looked around the expanse of the room. "Is there somewhere that isn't so . . . large? An office maybe?"

Ben nodded and led us through the main park office to a hall of individual offices in the back of the building.

"I'll start with Rylie, and then I'll come find you," Luke said to Ben. "We shouldn't be long."

Ben unlocked one of the doors leading to a modest office space. No pictures of family or trinkets littered the desk—only a small monitor, a keyboard and two chairs facing one another.

"This will be just fine." Luke offered me the more comfortable chair while he took the one opposite. The moment the door closed, his face widened into a smile. "How have you been, Ry? I can't believe you're here—I barely recognized you dressed like that."

I dropped my gaze and tried to control my smile. I couldn't tell whether my heart was racing because he was staring at me or because he was about to interrogate me.

"I've been, well, okay, I guess . . ." I picked at the hangnail on my thumb. My manicurist hated when I was under a lot of stress. She was always saying, "You no pick pick pick," in her Korean accent.

"I heard about you and Troy."

"Word travels fast." I couldn't meet his eyes. "Looks like you'll have to take sides. Don't worry, I won't be offended if you choose his side. I know the two of you played football together and went to academy together and—"

Luke reached across the desk and grabbed my hand.

"How could I take his side after what he did?"

I looked up into his deep brown eyes and frowned. "How do you know what he did?"

"He's been a tool since grade school. Plus, I've heard the rumors. Sucks that you lost your job and had to move in with your parents. I'm sure you miss the fire department a lot."

I nodded.

"Either way, you know I'll always be on your side." He ran a hand through his luscious brown hair. "We may have lost touch, but you've always been special—important to me."

And he had always been important to me too. We were high school sweethearts, prom king and queen, and when he proposed on graduation day in front of the entire senior class, I'm sure he thought it was a guaranteed yes.

But it hadn't been.

And as I sat across from him now, I could almost see that same look on his face—the one that indicated his heart breaking in front of ninety-seven of our closest friends.

"Anyway . . ." He looked down at his notebook and sat up a bit straighter. His heartbreak face melted into his professional face, and I knew what was coming next. "Can you tell me everything you remember about Ronnie Tilsdale?"

"Well, I haven't been here very long. Today's only my second day."

"That's okay, just start from the beginning."

I took a breath. "I had an interview with Ben on Thursday, and then I worked with him on Sunday, yesterday, for the closing shift."

Luke sat back and listened, nodding his head as if taking in every detail of my story. He had been a good listener when we dated too.

"Yesterday, I saw Ronnie with his wife. She was about as friendly as a mama moose."

"How do you mean?" Luke leaned forward and made a note in his notebook.

"When he started talking to me, she got out of the truck—all eight feet, three hundred and fifty pounds of her—and put him in his place. She looked like she was going to punch him."

Luke made another note. "Did Ronnie say anything that might have been important?"

"When Ben asked, Ronnie said he knew Dave and Clark fished back in the cove. I think he said Clark has been fishing somewhere else, but Ben and I saw Dave fishing back there yesterday morning."

"And did you talk to Dave?"

"Yeah, he was convinced Ronnie caught the catfish illegally and that he was setting the traps. He was even here when I interviewed, telling Carmen all about his suspicions. Saying how Ronnie better watch out or he might end up as dead as his catfish."

He scribbled furiously on his notepad then looked up at me. "Did you see anyone else fishing in the cove that day?"

"Jackson, one of the previous summer rangers, was back there. Other than that, no."

"Do you know Jackson's last name?"

"No, but I'm sure Ben does since he used to work here."

Luke nodded. "Go on."

"Then when we were closing up, we found Ronnie's body in the trap, and that's when we called you."

Luke leaned back. "This is very helpful, thank you."

"You're welcome. I'd be happy to help any other way I can." Ugh. Was I flirting?

"Any way?" He raised his eyebrow with a cheeky grin, his professional demeanor slipping away.

"Well, you know, so we can find Ronnie's killer." I looked down at my hands.

"Do you have any thoughts on who might have wanted him dead?"

"Maybe Dave. He seemed awfully peeved that Ronnie caught that catfish. And he did know about the traps. But so did Jackson, I guess. And Ronnie's wife seemed just mean enough and strong enough and crazy enough to do it." I shook my head. "I don't know, though. Maybe it was none of them."

I shrugged. Who was I to tell him how to do his job?

"Now about that offer. How about dinner?"

Butterflies I hadn't known still existed came to life in my stomach.

"I don't know, Luke. I haven't been single very long and—"

"Only to discuss the case," he added quickly. "You were always good at seeing what others don't. I could use your keen eye in this situation."

Nice excuse. We both knew he was far better at detective work than I had ever been, hence his degree in law enforcement and mine in parks and recreation. But at least it would get me out of the house for a night. "Okay, when?"

"I'm busy tonight, but how about tomorrow night?"

"Tomorrow night it is."

"I know the perfect place." He took out one of his business cards and wrote an address on the back. "It's a hole in the wall burger joint, but I think you'll like it."

Ben was waiting in the main office with Carmen when we reemerged. Luke went back to being the tight-lipped investigator, and I went back to training.

"You're lucky you missed the last hour," Shayla whispered when I sat down. "It was nothing but reminiscing on the good old days of rangering."

Had it really been an hour?

"Let's move on. Antonio, will you please hand out the radios?"

My head shot up so fast I nearly gave myself whiplash. Sure enough, there was Antonio, his piercing eyes on me as he handed Brock and Shayla radios.

"And one for you—the girl of my dreams," he said under his breath. I glanced over to see if Greg had heard him, but Greg was still futzing with the ancient projector screen.

Antonio winked at me and walked over to help Greg.

"Oh my gosh, did you hear that?" Shayla whisper-squealed next to me. Brock looked over with annoyance and then returned to playing with all the nobs and buttons on the radio in front of him.

"He's married," I whispered back.

Shayla blanched.

"These are training radios, so don't worry about accidentally calling out," Greg said giving up on the projector screen.

The radio in front of me was the exact model I'd used as a firefighter.

"When we call out, we go through several steps. First, you have to turn the radio on."

We all did as he showed. I could feel Antonio's gaze on me, but I refused to look at him.

"Then we make sure we have the correct channel. As you can see on the display it says R-1, which is our primary channel. If your display does not say R-1, you need to move the dials on the top to get to the appropriate channel."

Brock and Shayla ate up his every word, but I was daydreaming about Antonio and a burger and Luke. Had I really gotten over Troy so quickly? Just a week ago I had been convinced he was going to propose. That is, until I found him naked with giraffe girl. Tears welled in my eyes. Apparently, I wasn't completely over him.

"Rylie?" Greg's voice brought me back to reality. "You've used these radios previously, correct?"

"I have," I replied in the strongest voice I could find.

"Can you please demonstrate?"

"Sure." My heart quickened. I didn't want to make a fool of myself on my first day. Especially not in front of Antonio—not that I cared what he thought.

I steadied my hands and made sure the radio was on, and on the correct channel. "What's my call sign?"

"Oh gee, buddy. I haven't told you which ranger you are, have I?" Greg chuckled and shook his head. "That reminds me." He went to the desk where Antonio sat and pulled three badges out of a box. They were a bit tarnished—likely used by many previous summer rangers.

"Rylie, you're Ranger Fourteen." The badge—silver with a tiny number 14 on the bottom—was heavier than it looked. I pinned it to my uniform shirt. "Shayla, you're Ranger Fifteen, and Brock, you're Ranger Sixteen."

Brock looked especially irritated that he had the highest number on his badge.

"These were only assigned in accordance with the order in which you were hired. They have no relevance in the hierarchy." Greg looked at Brock when he said this.

"Okay, now go ahead, Rylie."

I took the radio and clicked the button on the side. "Ranger Fourteen, Ranger One?" My voice echoed through the room on each of the training radios.

Greg picked up his radio pretending as if I wasn't in the room with him. "Ranger One, go ahead."

I didn't know what he wanted me to say next, but he interrupted me.

"And then she would relay her message. I'm surprised you called it out correctly, though. Most agencies call it out opposite the way we do. We call out our personal call sign and then the person we're calling to."

He was right—the fire department did it the opposite way. "I heard Ben call out during my interview."

"Very good," Greg said.

Antonio smiled. I looked away.

"We do this because sometimes you won't hear who is calling, but you'll likely catch your own call sign when it's at the end."

Brock was writing notes furiously. Shayla picked at her

nails. How would they have reacted to seeing a dead body?

"Okay, Shayla, would you like to try?" Greg asked.

We each went through the motions of using the radio several times. Shayla and Brock had obviously never used a radio before, but by the end of the day they seemed to have gotten the hang of it.

"We'll reconvene tomorrow morning for more training. Rylie, you won't need to lock up with Ben tonight. We don't want to burn you out so early in the season."

Antonio followed us down the stairs and out into the parking lot. Shayla walked with me while Brock spewed questions at Antonio like a kid on too many packets of Fun Dip.

"Today wasn't too bad," Shayla said.

"Did you think it would be?"

She shrugged. "I didn't know what to think. My mom always made it sound like being in law enforcement was scary and challenging, both mentally and physically."

"I don't think this is real law enforcement—not like the police anyway."

Shayla reached up and twirled a long strand of curly blonde hair. "Sissy enforcement. That's what Mom called it when I told her I got the job. I've never been as tough as she is."

"It's not sissy enforcement. It's just different. This is a good way to dip your toe in," I said. "Plus, we get these stylish uniforms."

Shayla laughed and looked down at the stomach roll overtaking her belt. "We should all go out tonight and celebrate our first day."

"Can my wife come?" Brock asked.

"Uh . . . sure," Shayla said.

"I'll come for a bit." I smiled.

"Awesome." Shayla's face lit up. "I know the perfect place just down the road."

Antonio looked at me and quirked an eyebrow.

Nope. No way. I wasn't inviting a married guy out to the bar.

"You can come too, Antonio, if you'd like . . ." Shayla's cheeks blossomed as if she had been stung by angry red ants.

Antonio shrugged. "I'll see if I have plans."

I silently urged him to have plans.

I followed Shayla in her yellow Volkswagen Beetle straight from the reservoir to a little hole in the wall wings joint that was already crowded on a late Monday afternoon.

"I know the bartender." She ushered us through the crowd. "My mom always used to bring me here after her shifts."

"Your mom brought you to a bar?" I asked.

"Yep. Best wings in town."

Brock was still in his '91 Ford Taurus, talking on the phone.

"I hope Antonio comes," Shayla said over the crowd.

"I don't," I said under my breath. I knew his type. Always looking for something better. Never satisfied. He probably had a beautiful wife at home that he'd grown bored of, so he decided to hit on the summies. He was like a catfish to stink bait. Or a fisherman to catfish. I shook my head. It had only been two days and the job had already begun to permeate my thoughts.

The high-top table in the corner of the dimly lit bar was just big enough for the three of us. Near the door was a long bar with mirrors hung on the wall behind. Two tiny women moved effortlessly, slinging drinks to all the off-duty cops while neon signs lit their features.

"Shayla, Rylie, this is my wife, Bella." Brock stood next to the most adorable woman I'd ever seen. She was tiny with braided chocolate brown hair and matching puppy dog eyes surrounded by crazy long eyelashes.

"It's nice to meet both of you. I was so excited when Brock asked me to come along tonight."

Shayla and I were in shock. How could such a sweet woman be with such a tool?

"Uh . . . it's nice to meet you too," I finally said.

"Yeah, it is. Really nice." Shayla smiled.

"I'm so proud of him, you know?" Bella started as Brock took her jacket and pulled the stool out for her. "It was a huge blessing when he got the job. Even if it wasn't exactly what we hoped for, it'll help us pay the bills."

She looked at Brock as if he was Superman.

"Well, we're happy for him too," Shayla replied. "Should we order?"

We each ordered a beer from the tap and a bucket of "to-die-for" wings.

"I understand why your mom liked this place so much," I said to Shayla over the sound of voices and music. "It looks like there are mostly cops here."

"Yeah, I know most of them. They worked with Mom."

"Maybe you could put in a good word for me." Brock straightened up and glanced around while Bella held his hand and listened to the conversation.

"Uh, I'll see what I can do," Shayla said without looking up from her beer. "So Rylie, you were a firefighter?"

"Yeah, up in the mountains for Big Mountain Fire Department."

"It's gorgeous up there. Why'd you leave?" Shayla seemed sweet enough, but I wasn't about to go into my whole crazy history. Especially not in front of Brock and Bella.

"Just needed some space . . ."

"Running away from something, huh?" Brock asked.

"I guess you could say that." I sipped my beer. "But I like to think I'm running toward something better." What a load of cow shit. No way my parents' basement and a summer job with no room for advancement was better than my life had been in the mountains. Well, at least before I'd lost my job, found my boyfriend cheating, and realized I was the only one in the entire town who didn't know about his infidelity.

Brock chugged the rest of his beer. "We should probably go. Bella has an early morning tomorrow."

Bella nodded her head furiously. "I start my new job at the special needs preschool down on Tenth Street."

Wow. They were like polar opposites. But then Brock stood, helped Bella off the barstool and into her jacket.

"Thank you," she said and kissed him on the cheek.

"See you tomorrow," Shayla said.

The two of them made their way out of the bar with

Brock nodding at all the men he passed. Rookie was practically stamped on his forehead.

"He's quite the trip," Shayla said.

"I've seen the type, wants attention and thinks a badge
and gun will make up for his other . . . shortcomings."

Shayla nearly spat out her beer. "And what about
Bella?"

"Opposites attract, I guess." I shrugged.

"Maybe she knows something we don't . . ."

"Who knows." I raised my glass. "To first weeks."

She brought her glass up and clinked it against mine.
"To first weeks."

"Hear, hear!" A familiar voice behind me sent tingles
down my spine. "Hey, Shayla. Long time."

Shayla stood and wrapped her arms around Luke
—my Luke.

No. I couldn't think of him like that. You'd think after
all this time I'd have learned to let him go. There was no
way I could get involved with him again. I'd already done
too much damage there.

I watched in shock as he hugged her back and kissed
her on top of her head. "How's your mom?"

"Good. Enjoying retirement," Shayla sat back down.
"How's life without her?"

"Not nearly as entertaining," Luke said. He wore jeans
and a nice sweater with a button-down underneath. I
silently wished I'd worn something other than my
uniform pants and the plain navy blue t-shirt that went
under my button down uniform shirt.

"How do you know Rylie?" he asked, not looking at me
for more than a few seconds.

Shayla glanced at me and then back at him. "She's a ranger—a summer ranger—with me."

"Ah, so you got the job. That's great, Shay." He hugged her again. What was with all the hugging? And Shay? Really?

I knew I shouldn't be jealous, but did he really have to ignore me completely?

"Well, I'll leave the two of you to it," he said. "Have a good night." He walked over to the bar where he was greeted by the testosterone-laden sound of men cheering. Luke had always been Mr. Popular.

"So, how do you know Luke?" Shayla asked me.

"We dated in high school. It wasn't anything serious."

Recognition followed by disappointment washed over her face. "You're *Rylie*." She said my name as if it was a curse word.

"He talked about me?" I asked.

"Oh yeah, my mom heard all about the infamous Rylie. We actually joked that he'd made you up. He joined the force almost directly out of high school and was assigned as my mom's partner until she retired."

That explained their bond.

"He's a really great guy. I think you did a number on him."

"What do you mean?" I slipped a glance over at the bar where he stood, his back to me.

"As far as I know, he hasn't seriously dated anyone since you."

"But it's been years. There's no way—I'm sure he—"

"Nope, trust me, some of us would kill to have a guy

look at us like he looks at you." She motioned toward the bar where Luke now stood staring at us—at me.

"I should probably go. I have a long drive home." I stood from my chair and pulled on my favorite Denver Broncos hoodie. "Thanks for bringing me here. It was fun."

"No problem, we'll have to do it again sometime."

As I walked toward the door, I watched Shayla go right over to Luke and tuck herself under his arm. Her earlier timidity vanished in his presence. For the slightest moment, the jealousy returned until I ran smack dab into a wall.

At least, I thought it was a wall.

But when I looked up, the wall was strangely shaped like an Italian bodybuilder. Antonio stared down at me, a grin spreading across his face.

I took two steps back.

"Just the girl I was looking for." He took a step closer. "You're not leaving are you?"

"Yeah, I . . ." A bead of sweat trickled down my back.

"The Broncos, huh? You a fan?"

"Isn't everyone?" I let out a giggle like a schoolgirl and then silently chided myself for being such an idiot. What was it about me that was attracted to cheaters?

"We should catch a game together sometime."

I shrugged. The smell of his cologne was as intoxicating as his smile.

"Don't go." He draped an arm across my shoulders. "It looks like Shayla's made some friends. Let's go talk to them."

My head screamed objections, but before I could come

to my senses, we were standing face to face with a very confused-looking Luke, who still had his arm around Shayla.

Luke eyed Antonio and then me. My stomach sank.

"Hello again," Luke finally said, more to Antonio than to me.

The weight of Antonio's arm was starting to crush me. I shrugged him off. "I take it you've met?"

Antonio stuck out a hand and Luke took it, their knuckles white with effort. "He interrogated me today."

Of course, because Antonio and Kyle had been working that day too.

"It was more of an interview than an interrogation," Luke said. "Trust me. You'd know if you were being interrogated."

Shayla's eyes darted toward the door as the silence stretched out—the two men staring each other down.

"I've never seen you here before. What brings you to our hideaway?" Luke finally asked, grabbing a new beer from the bar and taking his arm off Shayla's shoulder. Her face dropped slightly.

"Shayla invited me. Said it was the place to be." Antonio's voice was deeper than it had been moments before.

I couldn't stand there anymore and watch their whose-is-bigger competition.

"I have to go. You guys have fun," I said with a quick wave to Shayla.

As I turned, Antonio caught my arm. "But you haven't even had a beer with us."

I pulled my arm away just in time to see Luke grab Antonio's wrist. "She said she had to go," he hissed.

Antonio yanked his arm from Luke's grasp. "Okay." He raised his hands in surrender. "Geeze. I didn't realize you two had a thing—"

"We don't," I spit out more quickly than I intended. A flash of hurt interrupted the anger dominating Luke's face, and my heart sank. Was it physically impossible for me not to hurt this guy?

"How about I go instead?" Luke said through gritted teeth. He grabbed his beer from the bar, chugged it down, and said goodbye to his friends and Shayla. When he brushed past me be growled, "You really know how to pick the winners."

I fought tears the whole way home. I had to explain myself. I picked up my phone a dozen times to text Luke. To tall him how Antonio and I were not a thing. How we would probably never be a thing being as Antonio was married. But every time I chickened out and set my phone back on the passenger seat.

I'd tell him everything at dinner tomorrow.

That is, if he showed up.

4

W riting practice tickets and learning park rules could not beat out the niggling deep down in my gut the next day. Why did I care so much what Luke thought? I knew the truth, and that was all that mattered. Wasn't it? Plus it wasn't like we were going to back together or anything.

"I just hope my face doesn't swell up too badly," Shayla said as we finished up lunch. At least she wasn't mad at me from last night. "My mother will never let me live it down if I can't handle a simple hit of pepper spray."

Her mother sounded like an ass.

At lunch, Greg had reminded us that we'd have a pepper spray drill that afternoon. As a firefighter, I'd never had to deal with pepper spray, but I'd heard horror stories about how it made some people physically sick. "It probably won't be so bad. Just get through the course and get to the hose, and it's all over," I patted her on the back. She flashed me a grateful smile.

Brock walked toward the test area with his shoulders back, eager to offer himself up as the first volunteer.

"All right, Brock, the minute Kyle sprays your face, time will begin," Greg explained. "You will first run across the plaza and get through the mob of park visitors without trampling anyone." He motioned to where Ben and Antonio stood acting as park visitors. "Then you will run across the beach down to the boat ramp, pick up the radio and call out for help, before we'll offer you the hose."

It sounded simple enough. We all nodded.

"Are you ready?" Greg asked.

Brock nodded once.

Kyle sprayed a quick burst of the toxic vapor directly at Brock's face. At first it seemed as though Brock was completely unfazed, but as he began running across the plaza he nearly tripped over his own feet rubbing furiously at his eyes. A moan of pain escaped his lips.

"Don't rub your eyes, that'll make it worse," Greg called out. "Keep going, you need to call for help. The assailant is getting away."

But no amount of coaxing got Brock back on track. He huddled on the ground in the fetal position clawing at his face, spewing expletives, and begging for water.

Shayla stared at him with her massive eyes.

At this point, even I was ready to give him my water bottle.

Finally, Kyle yanked Brock from the ground and shoved a water bottle in his hands. Brock dumped the contents on his face and reached for another.

"Who wants to go next?" Greg asked in his cheery

voice as if there wasn't a man still clawing at his eyes in pain behind him.

Shayla looked like she was going to vomit.

"I'll go," I said.

"Ready?" Kyle asked, his voice pulling me back to the task.

I took a deep breath and nodded.

The spray hit my closed eyes like a burst of cool steam. At first, it wasn't so bad, but the minute I opened my eyes to see where I needed to run, a burning sensation convinced me my corneas were being ripped out. I fought the urge to rub my eyes and blinked furiously.

"Go, Rylie." Shayla's voice reminded me of all the people watching.

I took a step and then two and then began running. I was across the plaza in a matter of seconds and into the crowd.

"Excuse me," I said as I gently pushed past Ben and Antonio. The beach was more difficult to maneuver as tears rolled down my face. My boots and heavy pants made it nearly impossible to run through the sand.

Once on the boat ramp, I searched frantically for the radio. I could only see shapes, and even those were blurry. The burning sensation was getting worse. I needed the water. Where was that damn radio?

Finally, I found it by the fishing regulation sign.

"Ranger Fourteen, Ranger One," I called out.

"Go ahead," Greg replied.

"A man about five foot eight with dark brown hair has taken my pepper spray and used it against me. He's headed in the direction of the plaza."

"Copy, I'll head that way," Greg replied.

"Ranger Fourteen clear," I said and put the radio down.

"Here you go." Carmen stood next to me with the hose spewing wonderful cold water. How had I not seen her there just moments before? "Let it run over your face and into your eyes. It'll make it feel better."

The cool water was like a slushy on a hot summer day. It slowed the burning on my cheeks and in my eyes. After a solid five minutes of cold water, the pain subsided to that of a severe sunburn.

Shayla was next and, though the pepper spray seemed to give her more problems than it had me, she made it through the course and was soon dousing her face with the hose.

"Great job, you two," Greg said in his cheery voice. "Rylie, you beat the record time." He clapped me on the back.

How had I beaten the record time? It took me forever to find the radio.

"And Brock, we'll give you the opportunity to take the test again, or you can simply go through the season and not carry the pepper spray."

Brock's entire face was swollen and purple. It looked as though he'd been stung by a hoard of angry bees. He nodded, silent.

"Shayla and Rylie, you can officially carry pepper spray." He handed us each a new can, which we placed in the empty holsters on our belts. "Congratulations."

Had I remembered pepper spray training would be the same day as my non-date with Luke, I'd probably have tried to schedule the non-date for another day. I took one last look in the mirror of the office bathroom and conceded that my eyes would remain a bright shade of red. Maybe my pitiful appearance would gain me a bit of sympathy.

"Whoa, where are you going?" Carmen asked.

I looked down at the skirt and blouse I'd traded my uniform for.

"You got a date, huh?" She smiled at me. "Is it that cute cop who was here the other day? I saw the way he was lookin' at you."

"Is it too much?" I smoothed my skirt down.

"Nah, girl, you look great. Well, minus those eyes."

"Did I hear someone say something about a date?" That Italian voice came from behind me. I spun around so fast, I almost fell in my heels, but Antonio was there. He slipped his arm around my lower back to steady me.

"I'm good." I removed myself from his grasp.

"Rylie here's got a date with that hunky cop," Carmen said with a giggle. "If I wasn't married, I'd have a piece of that myself."

Antonio looked me up and down. "The guy from last night? I thought you said you didn't have a thing."

"We don't anymore. I screwed it up years ago." I turned away. "See you guys tomorrow."

"See ya," Carmen called out. The door clicked into place behind me, and I let out a breath. Why did I let that man, that *married* man, get under my skin?

"Wait, wait," Antonio called from behind me. I picked

up speed, acting like I hadn't heard him, but my heels slowed me down and he was next to me within seconds.

"Why don't you like me?" He reached up and tucked a stray strand of hair behind my ear.

I looked directly into his honey-brown eyes. "Because you're married," I said with as much exasperation as I could manage.

He put his hands in his pockets and rocked back on his heels. "Ah, didn't know you knew that."

"Yep, I know. And I think it's shitty that you'd treat your wife with such disrespect."

"My wife? Disrespect?" He let out an exasperated noise. "My wife is a horrible, terrible monster of a woman who makes my life a living hell."

"Then get divorced." I started walking again, but he walked right alongside me.

"Oh, get divorced. It's that easy, is it?" He took a step closer. "If we got divorced I'd get nothing. I'd be homeless and penniless."

So she was the breadwinner. "I'd rather be homeless and penniless than in a relationship I couldn't stand." I could feel the word hypocrite spreading across my forehead. If Troy, or rather giraffe girl, hadn't kicked me out, I would have probably stayed there until the end of time.

"I'll let you get on with your date."

"Thanks." I turned and walked away as quickly as I could, my heart pounding in my chest like a bass drum.

My emotions regarding Antonio hovered somewhere

between extreme irritation and empathy. I knew how it felt to have a terrible significant other, to feel like you couldn't leave without starting over. But that didn't mean he had any right to hit on me. By the time I reached the burger joint, I was ready to jump out of my skin.

How dare Antonio ruin this non-date for me? Especially after he screwed everything up last night.

No, I wouldn't let him. I squared my shoulders and walked inside with a big smile.

The smile drooped when I saw the scowl on Luke's face. I waved half-heartedly and walked over with as much grace as I could muster. At least he hadn't stood me up.

"Sorry about my face." I sat down in the chair across from him.

"Pepper spray training, I suppose?" His voice was bored, unconcerned.

Of course he'd know.

"And I'm sorry about last night, it's not what you—"

He held up a hand. "Don't. It's none of my business. We're here to talk about the case, so let's stick to that, okay?"

Damn, he was sexy when he was mad.

The burger joint consisted of a whopping six tables— five of which were empty—and a grill in the back. It smelled heavenly, like grease and fat and meat, and it reminded me of the firehouse. A pang of sadness punched me in the gut. It seemed like an eternity since I'd fired up the grill for the weekly Saturday afternoon BBQ . . . since I'd had any control over my life. And how could I even think about dating someone as wonderful as Luke when my life was in such shambles? It wouldn't be fair to either of us.

We sat in silence studying the grease-splotched menus before the waitress came to take our order: a dumpster fire burger and sweet potato fries for me, and a moo moo burger and curly fries for Luke.

"Good to see you still have your appetite," Luke said with a hint of a smile.

"How's the case coming?" I asked, trying to stay on topic. "Any new developments?"

"We interviewed the wife today," Luke said. "She's strange, but I don't think she did it."

If I had to guess, she'd be exactly the person who could have done it, but again, he was the detective.

"Did she have an alibi?"

"She said she was at home the entire afternoon. She thought Ronnie was there too since she made him go home, but when she went out to their garage he was gone."

"Is there someone who can corroborate her story?"

"Corroborate?" The corner of Luke's mouth twitched like it always had when I'd say something amusing. "Big word, ten points."

So he remembered our point game. "What does that make the score now? Seven thousand, four hundred, fifty-four to forty-six?" I, of course, had the high score.

"It's been ten years. I think we should start a new game."

"Deal." I smiled.

He, on the other hand, retrained his face into a scowl.

"You didn't answer my question," I said. "Was there

someone to verify that she was at the house when Ronnie was killed?"

"Her neighbors gave statements that they saw Ronnie leave in his truck, but that his wife wasn't with him."

"She could have snuck out." I was grasping.

"I would doubt that woman could go anywhere without people noticing."

If Bigfoot could do it . . .

"Did you find his friend, Clark? Or talk to Dave? Or Jackson?"

"Slow down. We're getting there."

"Okay, so we have Dave, Clark, and Jackson." I counted on my fingers.

"Yes, and anyone else who may have been in that cove that day. Bikers, joggers, random passersby."

"That leaves, like, everyone." This investigation was going nowhere. It was like finding a needle in a haystack or catching a state record catfish: nearly impossible.

Luke nodded. "Investigation is a process. At least we've removed his wife as a suspect."

"Even though she doesn't have a strong alibi," I muttered under my breath.

"Here you go." The waitress set two plates of burgers and fries in front of us. "Need anything else?" She batted her eyelashes at Luke and he smiled back.

"Nothing else, Trish, thanks." She turned to leave.

Trish. Ugh. I bet those eyelashes were fake, along with . . .

"I'm not dating Antonio. He's married." I blurted out.

"I don't want to talk about this," Luke said. "Eat before your burger gets cold."

The burger in front of me was massive. Cheese and pickles and jalapeños and onion rings oozed with special sauce from beneath the toasted sesame seed bun. Challenge accepted.

No amount of milk could quench the fire that burned from my mouth all the way to my stomach, but it was worth it. Luke was right. This place had awesome food. If only *Trish* wouldn't come around to flirt.

"That was delicious," I said fighting the urge to unbutton my jeans. "They could call it the pepper-spray burger."

"I thought you'd like it." Luke smiled before he remembered he was supposed to be mad at me and turned his smile back into a frown.

"Oh, come on, how long are you going to be mad? I already told you, there's nothing between Antonio and I. I was leaving when he pulled me back in last night. And I'm . . ."

Luke raised his eyebrows. "You're what?"

"I'm, well . . . nothing, never mind. It's just that I'm not going to fall for someone I work with, that would be stupid."

"Okay, I'll drop it," Luke said. Always the forgiving one. "But I need you to do me a favor."

"What kind of favor?" My heart sped up.

"I need you to be my eyes and ears at the reservoir, provided you can stay out of trouble . . ."

What did he mean by that? "But I'm not—"

"Not what? Intelligent and observant? Yes, you are. And I can't be in all places at once."

He had a point.

"I'll do what I can, but no promises. With training and everything—"

"That's fine. I just want you to observe anyway. If something happens, call me. I don't want you placing yourself in harm's way." He smiled and my insides turned to mush. "And one more thing."

"Yes?" I leaned forward and smiled my sweetest smile.

"Can you watch out for Shayla?"

He may as well have punched me in the stomach.

I sat back and crossed my arms over my chest. "Sure, no problem."

"Oh, don't be that way. Shayla is—"

"Can I get you anything else?" *Trish* asked, her eyelashes fluttering a million miles an hour. That was it. My patience flew out on the breeze of her flutter.

"Just the check," I said. "Separate checks. Thanks."

"I was going to get it," Luke started.

"Don't worry about it. Like you said, it wasn't a date. We just had to discuss the case, which we did. And I should probably be getting home. I have training in the morning." I dropped a twenty on the table and stood up.

Luke nodded, disappointment etched in his forehead.

"I'll let you know if I hear anything. And I'll watch out for Shayla," I said with a forced smile before I walked away. Clearly, how he felt meant more to me than I'd thought. Not that I'd admit that to him.

5

"Get your pretty head out of bed." My mother's voice pierced my dreams.

I was riding a giant catfish through the air chasing Ronnie's killer as Antonio and Luke floated behind. Weird.

"Hello? Are you awake in there?"

I looked at the time on my clock. 6:45 AM.

Nope. No way. Even Fizzy didn't open his eyes next to me.

I pulled the comforter over my head and silently begged her to go away.

"Come on, open up. I have a surprise for you." Her voice was eager, giddy.

"Okay, okay." I got up and pulled a sweatshirt over my cami. "What's up?"

I opened the door and there stood my mother with the most beautiful thing I'd ever seen in her arms. My uniform was washed, pressed, and neatly folded. Maybe living at home wasn't so bad after all.

"Mom, you're the best!" I took the clothes from her and hugged them to my chest. Somehow, she had managed to get the stink out of the hat and the stains out of the shirt.

"I took in the pants a bit too. Didn't want anyone to see your underwear, or lack thereof." She mumbled the last part.

"It's a thong, which is still considered underwear."

"Underwear is designed to cover your under parts, a thong clearly does not cover your under parts."

Were we really having a conversation about my under parts this early in the morning?

"Well, thank you. I really appreciate it."

"Good. Now go upstairs and have some coffee before you leave. There are donuts too."

Was I in the Twilight Zone? Had my parents' home suddenly become Heaven?

"And do the dishes before you leave. They're starting to pile up. Bye."

And we're back to reality.

Four donuts and two cups of coffee later, I was in my like-new uniform and ready for the day. It's amazing what a good-fitting pair of pants and a decent hair day will do for your confidence.

The early summer breeze blew through my windows as I blared the radio and sang along. I pulled Cherry Anne into the parking spot by the shop, ran my fingers through my tangled hair then pulled it into a pony before threading it through the back of my dishwasher detergent-smelling hat.

"Hey, where'd you get a new uniform?" Shayla asked when I walked into the room.

"My mom made some alterations."

"It's unnatural to look that good in such an ugly piece of clothing." She shook her head. "Think your mom can fix mine too?" She looked down at her too-tight shirt, the buttons straining to hold the two sides together over her belly.

"I can ask her." I was sure she'd welcome the challenge and the attention. "Why don't you come to my house after training today?"

"Sure! Sounds fun." It was impossible to hate Shayla, even if Luke had some weird connection with her that raised my hackles. She was so sweet and unassuming.

"So you're the bitch who broke my record?" A high-pitched voice stabbed at my ears.

I whipped around to see a woman tall enough to be a model and beautiful enough to give Gal Gadot a run for her money. Her flowing auburn hair sparkled in the sunlight, and if it hadn't been for the evil glare on her face, I'd think she was a fairy-tale princess.

Shayla and I looked at each other, unsure who she had been talking to.

"Rylie, right?" The redhead stuck out her hand and shook mine with ferocity.

"I don't know about bitch, but yeah, I'm Rylie. And this is Shayla."

She shook Shayla's hand without taking her eyes off me.

"And you are?" I asked.

"Nikki, Ranger Twelve." She pointed to the badge pinned to her perfectly pressed uniform. I silently thanked my mother for my own wrinkle-free state.

"What record are you talking about?"

"The pepper spray course record. I've held it five years running."

"Er—sorry?"

"Oh you will be," she hissed.

"What?" Was she threatening me?

"Oh good, you've met Nikki," Greg walked in and looked around. "We'll wait for Brock, and then we can get started."

"I can't wait to take the boats out today!" Nikki's entire demeanor went from snake to bunny rabbit.

A knot formed in the pit of my stomach. I had absolutely zero experience driving a boat.

"Nikki has been a summer ranger for five years, and she's quite adept at boating, so she will be helping with training today."

Of course she was 'quite adept' at boating. I tried not to roll my eyes but failed.

"I'm here. I'm here." Brock burst into the room gasping for air. "Sorry I'm late. Traffic was shit."

"Not at all, Brock. We were just discussing boat training for the day."

Brock's face drained of color. "Boat training?"

"Yes." Greg sounded way too excited. "Since you will primarily be assigned to our three reservoirs, you will need to know how to operate our boats."

He droned on for a few minutes about patrolling on water and how we still had to check licenses and talk to fishermen. Once he was done with his speech, he showed us how to connect the pickup to the trailer, drive it down to the docks, and launch it into the water. Then we all left the security of dry land and boarded the two massive patrol boats. At least they were bigger than the boat my dad had when I was growing up. The one that only went about five miles an hour.

I was on one boat with Shayla and Nikki, of course, and Brock and Greg were on another.

Nikki threw a couple of life jackets at us, and we eagerly buckled them on. Greg and Brock sped off, leaving our lives in Nikki's hands.

"Greg wants me to show you the ropes and then give you each a chance to kill us. Do either of you have any experience on a boat?"

We both shook our heads.

"Perfect. Every year, they hire the idiots who know nothing."

Before I could throw back some witty retort, she jammed the throttle down making the front end of the boat rise up out of the water and the engines roar. It was all I could do to grab a handhold before we were tearing across the pristine glass water.

Shayla, thankfully, had found a seat and was holding on to the side of the boat for dear life. Nikki threw her head back and laughed. Her hair flowed dreamily in the wind. Gag me.

Finally, we came to where Greg and Brock had

stopped, and Nikki pulled the stick back into a vertical position, bringing the boat to a perfect stop right next to Greg's.

"Very nice, Nikki. It seems you haven't lost your touch," Greg praised.

"I get lots of practice with our family boats on Lake Powell." Her tone was once again sugary sweet, and her smile as white as the fluffy clouds.

"First thing we need to do is discuss how boats are operated. As you see, the throttle is the stick on the right of the steering wheel . . ."

Greg went over every aspect of the boat while I wished I had put on more sunscreen and worn sunglasses. The sun was bright and my skin was scorching. By the time my turn to operate the boat came around, I could barely move my crispy limbs.

"Okay, now gently push the throttle forward," Nikki said, still in her sweet voice as Greg was watching. "Good job, Rylie."

She slapped me on the back with a bit more force than necessary. My whole body tensed. How dare she touch me?

"Now, I want you to make a circle out in the open water and come back to the side of Greg's boat."

It didn't seem so hard at first. There was no breeze, and the boat seemed to respond to every motion I made. That was, until I tried to come up beside Greg's boat. I turned the wheel too late, and the nose of the boat almost careened into the side of the other boat. Nikki pushed me to the side and took the controls, expertly maneuvering the boat in a way utterly foreign to me. Score one point for Nikki. I sat down, furious with myself that I hadn't done a better job.

"Not bad for your first try, Rylie," Greg said with his unending enthusiasm. "How about Shayla takes a turn now?"

Nikki handed the wheel over to Shayla, and she too had troubles maneuvering the boat. When Brock's turn came, he accidentally pushed the throttle forward rather than backward, and his boat plowed into the side of ours.

"Dammit." Brock threw his arms in the air.

"That's what the bumpers are for," Greg consoled. "Don't worry, you'll get the hang of it."

"When hell freezes over," Nikki whispered.

"Okay, why don't we go back into the coves and have a look around?" Greg said. And he and Nikki both jammed the boats into forward motion. This time we all knew what was coming and held on.

The coves were nearly empty. Fishermen dotted the shoreline, and there were two or three boats, but otherwise, the reservoir was completely peaceful.

"Who can tell me which cove this is?" Greg asked.

Nikki smiled and raised her perfectly manicured hand.

"Of course you can, Nikki. Anyone else?"

Shayla tentatively raised her hand. "Muddy Water Cove?"

"Very good," Greg said. "It looks different from this angle, doesn't it?"

Without the dead body and catfish traps? Yeah, it looked different. I squinted to see the spot from where we'd pulled the traps. The water was completely undisturbed. Maybe Ronnie had been the MWB after all.

"Isn't this where they found Ronnie's body?" Nikki asked.

"Yep, Ben and Rylie were the ones to recover it." Greg smiled at me.

"Do they have any leads on who the killer might be?"

"You're talking to the wrong person. As I hear, Rylie's been pulled into the investigation. She knows one of the investigators assigned to the case."

Nikki's look of pure hatred hit me like a freight train.

"Nothing new, I'm afraid." I wasn't about to let her in on the investigation, no matter how scary she was.

Each of us was given several more opportunities to operate the boats. We practiced approaching buoys as if they were other boats, keeping the boat steady while we pretended to check licenses, and then drive away without running over the buoy. I definitely wasn't an expert by the end, but I could probably manage to not kill anyone with the boat by the time we were done.

"Ranger Two, to all Ranger staff," Kyle's voice came from our radios.

"Go ahead," a voice that I hadn't heard on the radios much, replied.

"We are all needed in the training room at Alder Ridge stat."

"Five and I are pretty far out," the voice was deep and smooth. "You sure we need to be there?"

"Ursula requested all of our presence."

"Copy. Be there with bells on."

"Sounds like we need to head back to the docks," Greg said, a look of panic shadowing his face.

Nikki nodded and they both idled out of the cove. As

we floated past the other boats and shore fishermen, Greg waved and the fishermen waved back. They all seemed to respect and like the rangers rather than fear them.

I sat next to Shayla and watched the shoreline. As we reached the part where the Ronnie had been found, a figure stood in the trees. The same shape and size as someone I knew. Ronnie's wife.

I had to get back there to talk to her. Luke might be sure she wasn't the one who offed her husband, but I was still convinced she was our prime suspect. Lunch would be the only free time I could sneak back there, but Cherry Anne was prohibited from driving around the trails, and I hadn't been given rein to drive the patrol trucks yet. I would have to drive around outside the park and find the gate in the neighborhood behind the reservoir, but I wouldn't have a ton of time to talk to her once I found her. Hopefully, whatever this Ursula woman had to tell us wouldn't take long.

By the time we reached the dock, I was growing impatient. Ronnie's wife could be anywhere by now. She was probably gone.

Nikki expertly backed the boat into the slip and I yanked off my life jacket, handed it to her, and took a wobbly step onto the dock.

I started to walk, but my boots slipped in a pile of goose poop, my arms went flailing, and I landed ass-first in the shallow water next to the dock.

I stood as fast as I could, trying not to submerge myself entirely, but it was no use. I was drenched.

"Oh, oh my!" Greg splashed into the water after me. "Here, take my hand."

He helped me up and back onto the sandy beach where Nikki and Brock stood, not even trying to hide their amusement. So much for my perfect uniform.

When we reached the training room to grab our stuff for lunch, we were met with an entire room full of people.

"Welcome," a woman as tall as she was wide with long black hair said from the front of the room.

Sitting at our desks were Antonio, Ben, and Kyle.

"Please, take a seat. We're still waiting on the trail rangers."

My shoes squeaked all the way to my seat, and a puddle formed around my chair as I sat.

"Boating accident?" the woman asked in a grating voice.

"Oh no, n-nothing like that," Greg stammered, his voice far from its usual happy tone.

Nikki spoke up, "Rylie just tripped on her own feet and fell into the water next to the dock."

"Rylie, are you all right?" the woman asked.

"Yeah, I'm good." I smiled as sincerely as possible. Who was this woman again?

"Great."

No one moved. They all seemed petrified of this roly-poly woman.

"Let me introduce myself while we wait. I am Ursula Vilago, the city's Director of Parks and Recreation."

This woman was the big Kahuna, the head honcho, and effectively my boss.

"It's a pleasure to meet you," she nodded in turn to me, Brock, and Shayla. "And it's good to have you back, Nikki."

"It's good to be back," Nikki said in her saccharine voice.

The guys all stared down at the table in front of them. What was going on? Why were they all acting like scared puppies?

Then the door opened and two rangers walked in like they were in an action movie, strutting out of an exploding building. One, scruffy with brown hair and a stocky athletic build, pulled off his aviator glasses and threw a short nod to the other rangers. The other, tall, dark and gorgeous in a Calvin-Klein-underwear-model way, smiled showing the whitest teeth I'd ever seen.

"I'm glad you were able to join us," Ursula said in a voice that didn't convey even the slightest bit of joy.

"We were out on a trail, so it took us a bit longer to get here," the first one said as they took seats in the back of the room.

"Very well, I will get on with it since I have several other meetings this afternoon." She straightened her white blouse and squared her shoulders. "We are going to be making some changes to the ranger group."

Every head shot up to look at her.

"We have been given additional funds to increase staffing." She spit out these words as if they were bitter in her mouth. "As soon as possible, we will be hiring an additional full-time ranger."

I could almost hear Nikki's heart beating as she sat up straighter and flashed her big grin at Ursula.

"Of course, we'd like to hire from within and will be considering our summer rangers first. However, if we do not find one who can meet the qualifications, we will have to look outside the organization."

A sigh of relief went through the full-time rangers.

"The reason we will be hiring an additional ranger is that we will be hosting several programs and events that require a ranger's oversight. We would like this new hire to be the point person for those programs and events."

Nikki looked like she might fall off the edge of her seat. I couldn't blame her—a part of me was excited too. Though I was sure she'd get it over me.

Either way, I had to try.

"Are there any questions?"

Nikki's hand shot up. "I would *assume* seniority would provide some of us an upper hand?"

Ursula cracked what I guessed to be her version of a smile, though it looked more like a grimace. "Yes, Nikki. Your assumption is correct."

Great. So I had no shot.

"Barring any new developments, that is. I don't want to discourage any of you," she motioned toward Shayla, Brock, and me, "from applying and working hard to prove yourselves."

Maybe if I helped solve the murder, she'd consider me more seriously. I looked down at my soaking pants. Or maybe not.

"If there are no other questions, I'll take my leave."

She waited for a second, gathered her briefcase, and left without another word.

"That's it?" One of the trail rangers murmured behind me. "That's what we had to come all the way here for?"

"At least it's not what we thought," Ben replied. "We still have a ranger program."

Wait, they were worried she would shut the program down altogether? How could they have such nice trucks and facilities and still be worried about losing their jobs?

"Looks like they've decided we're valuable after all." Greg smiled. "And one of you may be joining us permanently."

His eyes swept over us and rested on Nikki.

Antonio winked at Nikki and she blushed. My chest tightened. Of course they'd have a history. She had been a summie for five years, and hadn't Ben said Antonio has a thing for summies?

"But programs and events? We have enough going on without adding more to the mix," Kyle chimed in.

"Hey, if it brings in money and gives us another full-time position." Antonio smiled at Nikki. "It'll make us even more valuable."

My leg began to shake impatiently. I didn't want to, couldn't sit here watching Antonio flirt with Nikki while Ronnie's wife might still be out there. If I had any chance at all at getting the full-time gig, I needed to solve this murder.

"Can I take lunch now?" I asked.

"Of course," Greg replied. "Be back in an hour, okay?"

"Okay." I was up and out the door before anyone could stop me, squishy boots and all.

It took almost half an hour to wind through the maze of houses and find the right gate. There were no vehicles parked there, but Ronnie's wife could have gone on foot or bike. I trudged out of my Mustang, leaving a huge wet spot on the seat that resembled the time I'd lost control of my bladder in Troy's truck on the way home from a particularly awesome concert. His reaction, however, had not been all that awesome.

"Sorry, Cherry Anne. I'll clean it up when I can." I shook my head. Stop talking to your car and get in the game.

I needed to figure out what I was going to say when I found Ronnie's wife. Luke would probably want me to call him, but it wasn't like I was going to interrogate or interview or whatever. I was simply taking a walk on my lunch break.

My boots were still sopping wet when I got to where Ben and I had pulled the trap from the water. Footprints the size of Sasquatch's led down to the shoreline, but not back up. My pulse raced. She was still down here.

The trees where I'd seen her before were empty, but her footprints led farther down the shoreline. I picked up speed. Time was running short.

I continued down the sandy shoreline until my time was up. I barely had ten minutes to get back to my car and find my way out of the neighborhood maze. I sloshed my way out of the park, my thighs now severely chafed by my wet cargo pants.

When I was almost out of the gate, something caught my eye—something poking out of a trashcan.

It was a loop of rope, purple and green—exactly the colors of the rope fibers that were found in Ronnie's strangulation marks. How had Luke and the others missed this? It wasn't that far from the crime scene.

I pulled out a pair of gloves and tugged it from the trash. Luke needed to see this as soon as possible.

The rope was quickly and securely stored in the trunk of my car within a plastic grocery bag from my trunk. I took off the gloves and included them in the bag before slipping behind the steering wheel, sitting in a puddle of my own making, and starting the engine.

My disappointment in not finding Ronnie's wife was squelched though when I noticed a piece of paper tucked under one of my windshield wipers.

Meet me tonight. 8:30. Here. Come alone.

The handwriting wasn't distinguishable as male or female, but the message was clear.

6

My tires squealed as I pulled up to the shop and dashed back into the training room. Completely breathless and still reminiscent of a drowned rat, I came face to face with the two gorgeous and still unknown-to-me rangers.

"Oh, sorry," I said between gasps for air. The two bad boys of the group stood before me with looks of amusement on their faces.

"Nice to meet yeh, Rylie," the scruffy one said in a distinct Irish accent. "I'm Seamus, and this here's Dusty."

"Sup?" Dusty lifted his chin slightly.

Seriously, how many hot guys did they hire here? They could have their own calendar.

"Yeh probably won't see us much. The reservoirs aren't our jurisdiction," Seamus said. "But join us on patrol every now and again to learn about the trails, if yeh like."

Behind him, Antonio's eyes shifted from a very chatty Nikki to giving Seamus' back the evil eye.

"I'll do that, thanks."

They both nodded and left as suavely as they'd come. If they were looking for someone to complement their GQ brand, they'd definitely want Nikki over me. I sighed and returned to my seat, happy my tardiness had gone unaccounted for.

"Hey, I'm having another Avs party this week if you want to come," Antonio said to Nikki in a louder than necessary voice. Then he turned to the room. "And Brock and Shayla, you can come too. The more the merrier."

"Isn't your wife going to be there?" Nikki wrinkled her nose.

He ignored her and glanced over at me. I looked away. If he thought I was going to beg for an invitation, he was sorely mistaken.

By the time training had finished, I was unimaginably chafed and exhausted. The last thing I wanted to do was have Shayla over to hem her clothes before I needed to sneak out and meet whoever had left that note on my car. But I had promised.

"I'll just follow you, okay?" As we got into our cars, her cheerfulness almost made me smile.

It was no surprise my mother was all too happy to show off her mother-of-the-century skills and was instantly bustling around taking Shayla's measurements. While they worked on that, I took a hot shower and changed out of my disgusting water-logged uniform and into a pair of comfy jeans and a white t-shirt in hopes that Ronnie's wife wouldn't see me as the woman who her husband had flirted with, but more of an ally. At least until I could figure out if she was the one who killed him.

"Mom?" I called when I came up the stairs.

"Just in time. We're all done with Shayla's measurements, and I thought we could sit down and have some lasagna before I get to work on the alterations. They shouldn't take me too long."

I looked at the large clock on the wall. I still had time before I had to meet Ronnie's wife. "Okay. Do you mind if I throw my uniform in the wash?" I secretly hoped she'd wave her magic mom wand again and my uniform would be back to its like-new status in the morning.

"Go ahead. But make sure to use the right settings and add some other clothes to make a full load."

I did exactly as she asked. There were two things for which my mother didn't have grace: people who talked badly about her family and doing the laundry the wrong way.

"Do you find it frightening that Rylie found a dead body at the reservoir?" Mom asked as we dug into her homemade lasagna. Dad didn't say anything, but I could tell he was listening intently.

"Not really," Shayla replied. "My mom is a retired police officer so I'm sort of used to it."

"Shayla wants to be a police officer too."

Shayla beamed at me.

"Only if I lose some of this weight. Heck, I might need my uniform to be taken in by the end of the summer."

"You're perfect just the way you are," my mother cooed. "Don't let anyone tell you otherwise."

"Why can't my mom be as nice as yours?" Shayla asked.

I shrugged. If only she knew. "Maybe you should tell your mom how you feel. Maybe she'd lighten up some."

"Nah, she's hard core. Way tougher than I'll ever be."

"I think you're tough. I mean, look at how you took that pepper spray course. You killed it."

My mom's eyes widened at the mention of pepper spray, but she didn't say anything.

"At least I was better than Brock, right?" She smiled.

"I don't think that's giving yourself enough credit." I laughed. "Brock was awful."

"Do you think he'll make it to the end of the season?"

"I don't know. They probably need the warm body more than they need someone to be able to take a hit of pepper spray. Plus, he knows the code book backwards and forwards."

"That's true. He does." Shayla seemed to be cheering up. "And I heard him talking to Seamus. You know, the cute Irish one? I think they're going to take him with them on the trails a bit more this summer. It sounds like the trail rangers are way more laid back and less visible to the powers that be."

"I wouldn't mind hitting the trail with them . . ." I said with a mischievous smile.

"Me neither," Shayla replied and we both burst into giggles.

My dad excused himself from the table, and my mom

stood too. "I'll go finish up those alterations so you don't have to wait around for me all night."

"It's no problem. Your home is so cozy, and it's really nice to have a friend." Shayla looked at me with a thankful smile. I hadn't had a friend—a girl friend—in a really long time, and I could definitely do worse than Shayla.

"Are you going to apply for the full-time ranger position?" I asked when my parents had gone.

Shayla shrugged. "I don't know. There's no way I'd get it."

"I don't know that anyone has a shot over Nikki, but it'd be a good experience nonetheless."

"That's true. And really, what do I have to lose?"

"Exactly." I had nothing to lose either but so much to gain.

"Okay, I'm all done. As I said, there really wasn't much I needed to do, but I think this'll help." My mom came out of her sewing room with Shayla's uniform in her arms. "Now, I wrote down some instructions on how to get the stains out, and I'm sure your mother knows a thing or two about how to iron a uniform, but if not, feel free to call me. My number's on there too."

"Wow, thanks Mrs. Cooper. You're awesome." Shayla held her uniform with the same gentle touch one would use holding a newborn baby.

I eyed the clock. Almost seven thirty. "Sorry to cut this short, but I have to be somewhere."

"You're going out? Tonight?" My mother frowned. "It's already so late."

"I have an errand to run, nothing big. Don't wait up though. Shayla, I'll walk you out."

"Okay, thanks again for my uniform. I can't wait to try it on."

Once we were in the driveway, I turned to Shayla, "I need to tell you something."

"Yeah?"

"I have to go somewhere tonight and it might be dangerous, but I have to go alone."

Shayla's eyes were huge. "Does this have something to do with the investigation? Because I really think you should call Luke and—"

"No, I can't call him. He could compromise my ability to obtain the information."

Shayla shook her head. "Never go alone." Her voice was filled with worry. "My mother's number one rule. Never go alone. You could get hurt and no one would know."

"That's why I'm telling you. So someone does know." I smiled. "It's almost as if I wasn't going alone."

"Then I'll go with you."

"No," I said too quickly. "I mean, you can't."

"Why not?"

"Because Luke would kill me if I put you in danger—not that I'll be in danger, but I can't risk . . ."

Shayla narrowed her eyes at me with her hands on her hips. "You don't have to protect me. I'm perfectly capable of protecting myself."

"That's not what I meant. I know you are, it's just that Luke asked me to watch out for you and—"

"He did?" Her eyes were wide, and her frown instantly transformed into a smile.

Of course she would perk up to hear that. What girl

wouldn't want a handsome guy who cared about her well-being? Especially one as wonderful as Luke.

"At least tell me where you're going."

"You have to promise you won't follow me or tell anyone where I am." I was running out of time if I wanted to get there early.

"Okay."

"I'll be at the park gate in the back of the reservoir that leads to Muddy Water Cove."

"I knew it. This has something to do with Ronnie's murder, doesn't it?"

"I don't know exactly. Maybe. Probably."

"You know, you're not going to prove anything to anyone by getting yourself killed trying to solve this murder. They can't hire a dead person for the full-time position."

Was I really that transparent?

"We already concluded that the job is Nikki's. I'm not trying to prove anything."

"Fine, but if I don't hear from you by ten o'clock tonight, I'm calling Luke and telling him everything."

It was the best I was going to get. I nodded.

At least now if something happened, they'd know where to find my body.

The sun was fading when I pulled up. It had been much easier to find this time. I parked a bit down the street, just in case someone recognized my car, and I hid in a patch of trees close to the gate. Then I waited.

A few fishermen and bikers left the park before the gate closed. Antonio and Kyle were on the closing shift. I couldn't help but hope to get a glimpse of Antonio when he locked the gate. Even if he was a pig, he was as hot as bacon straight from the griddle.

Thankfully the sight of a big black truck and a uniformed figure distracted my thoughts. A little piece of me was disappointed that Kyle was closing the gates for the night. But at least it kept me from thinking of one of my married co-workers as a delicious piece of meat.

"You have to stay away from her. She's just going to get you into trouble," Kyle said into his cell phone. I leaned forward. Who was going to get who into trouble? "Especially if she gets hired on full-time. Don't give her any leverage over you."

There was a pause before he continued. "Your wife is sexy too . . . in her own way. Maybe you should focus on her a bit more."

He pulled out his keys and swung the gate shut. "Welcome to marriage. Every wife is a nag. You chose her for some reason—Maybe you should find that reason again."

I was ninety-nine percent sure he was talking to Antonio. If so, his advice was spot on, yet a bit disheartening.

Luke. I need to focus on Luke. No. Not Luke either. Someone else. No one else. But definitely not Antonio. *Married* Antonio.

"Have you caught them?" He turned away from me and walked back to the truck. I strained to hear the rest of the conversation, but he was too far away.

The ranger truck rumbled to life and took off down the path. I tried to shake the conversation from my head.

There was no way I was going to get in between a man and his wife, no matter how much he said they were on the outs. Plus, he was talking about Nikki anyway. She and Antonio had been awfully flirty in the training room.

I sighed and glanced at my watch. 8:45. Where was Ronnie's wife? My eyes were finding it hard to focus in the dimming light, and I had a cramp forming in my left butt cheek from squatting so long.

When my watch read 9:00, I stood and stretched my legs. Had I really thought this was a good idea? Someone was probably just messing with me. It wasn't like I was an investigator.

The trek back to my car was harder than expected now that the dark had settled in and my butt was in full-on cramp mode. Once inside, I threw my cell phone onto the passenger seat and put the key in the ignition. If I hurried, I could make it home in time to see the ten o'clock news and notify Shayla that all was good so she wouldn't call Luke.

But before I turned the key over, another note caught my eye. Seriously? I grunted my way back out of the car and yanked the note from beneath my wiper.

Don't leave, he's coming.

A chill ran down my spine. Who was coming? And why the cryptic notes?

I glanced around at the houses up and down the street.

Cars were safely tucked away in massive garages, and only a few cars dotted the curbs. None looked terribly suspicious.

Pressing the note into my back pocket, I eased back toward my previous hiding spot. Halfway there, I spotted a shadow approaching the locked park gate. The person was decked out in black from head to toe and held what looked like a fishing rod and tackle box in his hand.

I reached for my phone to snap a photo but remembered I'd thrown it on the passenger seat of my car.

Of course I had.

When I turned back, a strong hand clasped over my mouth and pulled me backward, into the bushes.

My screams didn't escape the gloved hand, and whoever this was easily avoided my flailing arms and legs.

It was all over.

The killer knew I was looking for them. I'd be the next target. At least I'd told Shayla where to find my body. I could just picture her and Luke shaking their heads at my stupidity.

"Stop wigglin'. I'm not gonna hurt ya," a voice whispered in my ear.

I stopped.

"Now, promise ya won' be stupid and holler when I take my hand away."

I nodded. What choice did I have?

The hand slowly released me, and I tried to run. I wasn't fast enough, though. My captor pulled me back and spun me around.

Face to face with none other than the woman I thought I'd been there to see all along.

"Are you the one who left me the notes?"

"Sure am." Ronnie's wife nodded, proud of herself.

"Why?"

"Didn' ya see him?"

"The guy sneaking into the park? Yeah. But what does that matter?"

"He's the one puttin' out the traps. He—he's the one who catfished Ronnie."

I rocked back on my heels and tried not to laugh. Clearly she didn't know what catfished really meant. "Why didn't you tell the police about this?"

"I did but they didn' care. Prolly didn' believe me." Her eyes sparkled in the moonlight. "Plus, I thought you was a good one to tell when I saw ya here this afternoon cuz us ladies gotta stick together."

She hadn't seemed so keen on us ladies sticking together when we'd first met.

"Why were you here this afternoon?"

"I's spyin' o'course."

Either this woman was telling the truth, or she was a masterful liar. Only a small part of me believed her. And it wasn't the part that had just been lifted clean off the ground by this Sasquatch of a woman.

"What did you find when you were spying?"

"That—that man." She pointed to where the man had jumped the gate. "I dunno who he is, but he's breakin' the law."

"I didn't see a cage with him, though. And I was in the cove this morning. There wasn't a cage submerged."

"He coulda hid it a different time."

"Well, I need to call the police and the rangers and get them out here ASAP."

She nodded vigorously. "Good idea."

"My phone is in my—" The sound of sirens grew louder in the distance. Sure enough within seconds, two police cars tore around the corner with their lights flashing.

"How'd they know? What did ya tell 'em? I told ya to come alone."

Why she was panicking was beyond me. She had been on board with calling them a second ago.

"I didn't—no. I don't know how—" Then my eye caught the sight of a yellow Volkswagen.

Shayla.

"I'll take care of it," I said to Ronnie's wife, but when I turned to look at her she was gone. Vanished without a sound. Just like Bigfoot.

I'd catch up with her later. Right now, I had to find Shayla.

7

"What were you thinking following me?" I asked Shayla when she stepped out of the car.

"Oh, like you were being *so* safe coming out here on your own." She wrapped me in a bear hug. "I'm just glad you got away."

"Got away?" I patted her on the back.

"When I saw that person grab you and pull you into the bushes, I had no choice but to call the police. I mean, I guess I could have gone after you. Dang it, that's what I should have done. My mother would be so disappointed that I—"

"You did the right thing," I said. "And I'm glad you called them. Someone is trespassing in the reservoir and we—er—I think it might be the killer."

She quirked an eyebrow at my slip but let it go when Luke stepped out of his car.

The expression on his face was murderous.

"Look, I can explain, and I will, but right now, I need you to come with me." I grabbed his wrist and pulled him toward the gate. "Someone is trespassing in the reservoir, and I think it might be the killer."

"Why? What would make you think—"

"I just do, okay?"

Luke called out on the radio that he would be investigating a trespassing case at the Alder Ridge Reservoir and wouldn't need backup at this time. He and his partner led Shayla and me to the gate that still stood locked.

"Do either of you have keys to this gate?"

"Not with me," Shayla replied.

I shook my head.

"Perfect, I'll have to get the bolt cutters." He turned to go back to his car. "Shayla, come with me."

A pang of jealousy stole through me, but I pushed it away.

"So you saw someone go in there, huh?" Luke's partner asked.

"Yeah, a tall figure dressed in all black with what looked like a fishing rod and tackle box."

"And why exactly were you here tonight?"

"I got an anonymous tip," I said. Thankfully I hadn't told Shayla about the notes.

He let out a rolling laugh. "Who would send *you* an anonymous tip? You're just a park ranger, right?"

I didn't know whether to punch this guy or cover his mouth due to the booming of his laughter. Surely the trespasser would hear him and hide.

"Keep it down, Jerry," Luke said coming back toward

us, but instead of Shayla, Antonio was following him. "Do you want everyone to know we're here?"

"What—what's he doing here?" I asked.

"He heard me call out on the scanner and brought us keys."

Antonio winked at me. I pretended not to notice.

"Shall we?" Luke said through gritted teeth motioning toward the gate.

Antonio opened the lock. "It'd be better to go in with a vehicle, but it's not too far to walk."

"We can walk," Luke said. "Rylie, you stay here. In fact, go back to your car, or back to Shayla's and sit with her."

"But I saw the guy. I can help."

"No," Luke's voice was sterner than I'd heard in a long time. "If this guy is the killer, he'll have no qualms about killing again. I can't have you—" he ran a hand through his hair, "Just go back to the car."

I turned and huffed back to Shayla's car where she looked equally pissed to have been dismissed.

"What exactly did you tell him?" I asked as we leaned up against the hood of the emoji on wheels.

"I'm sorry, Rylie, I really am. I didn't want to tell him, but when you were pulled into the bushes, I didn't know what else—"

I took a breath. "I'm not mad. I just want to know exactly how much he knows."

"Everything." She hung her head. "I told him everything."

Perfect. He was going to ream me for this one.

We stood in silence for what seemed like an eternity

waiting for something to happen. A couple of cars passed, but one slowed and then stopped in front of us.

Kyle stepped out.

"I heard on the scanner there was a trespasser," he said.

"Yeah, the police and Antonio are already in there."

"Maybe I should go help too."

"Doesn't look like you'll need to. Here they come," Shayla said. And sure enough, four people were making their way from the gate and toward us.

When they got within the streetlamps, I could make out Antonio, Luke, Jerry, and Dave. The fisherman.

"Can you take us to your car, please?" Luke held Dave's arms behind his back, likely in cuffs.

"Truck, it's a truck, and it's over this way."

We all followed. He had parked almost two blocks away.

"Look, I was just fishin'. I know I'm not supposed to be here after dark, but it's when all them big-uns come out." Dave babbled on and on as we approached his pickup. "I dunno what you're looking for, but you ain't gonna find it—"

Antonio pulled a green and purple coil of rope from the bed. "What do we have here?"

Dave scrunched up his face to see. "Looks like rope to me. Not mine though. Someone musta put it there."

My stomach turned. The rope was the same as the piece I'd found in the trash.

"Er, Luke?" I said. "I have something else I need to show you."

Luke followed me back to my car as his partner searched the rest of Dave's vehicle.

"I cannot believe you'd be this stupid. Careless. You were supposed to call me to handle these things. And after I told you to watch out for Shayla, you bring her into this—this . . . situation."

Of course, he was mad that I'd endangered his poor, sweet Shayla.

"I told her not to follow me! And we caught the bad guy, didn't we?"

"There's a whole lot of evidence missing to pin the murder on Dave. A spool of rope in the back of his truck isn't enough—"

I pulled the bag out of my trunk and handed it to him. "I'd venture to guess that rope has Ronnie's DNA on it. And it matches the rope in his truck."

Luke's jaw dropped open. "Where did you find this?"

"I pulled it out of the trashcan just inside that gate." I pointed to the entry gate where they'd taken Dave out in handcuffs moments before.

"You . . ." He took the bag from my hand and looked inside.

I was ready for him to praise me for finding the murder weapon, but instead of his face relaxing into a smile, it became even tighter.

"I cannot believe you touched this, let alone put it in the trunk of your car. That could completely ruin our case."

"But I used gloves. I didn't touch it."

"You put it in a grocery bag in the back of your car. Any defense attorney is going to rip that evidence to shreds and put plenty of reasonable doubt in the jury's mind. And if you had called me I would have known that."

I fought back the tears forming in the corners of my eyes. My pride was shot.

"Oh, and Shayla called because she saw someone grab you. Mind telling me about that?"

"It was Ronnie's wife," I said in the strongest voice I could find.

"Patricia?"

I shrugged without meeting his eye. I'd never gotten her name.

"And why exactly did Patricia want to meet you here?"

"Because she knew about Dave. She said she told you, but you didn't take her seriously."

"It was a lead I was following up on. I don't usually give the general public details of my investigations."

"Well, I guess she trusted me a little bit more."

"Just last night you were convinced Patricia was the killer. Now she's your best buddy?" Luke shook his head.

He was right. Did one piece of rope that Dave claimed he'd never seen before mean he was the killer? Maybe she planted the rope in his truck to frame him.

"I'm not saying she's my buddy. She might still be the killer. She could have planted that evidence."

Luke threw his hands in the air. "You're impossible." He started walking back toward the others.

"No, stop. Listen to me." I grabbed his arm and he turned back to look at me. "If Patricia knew Dave would be there, she could have easily put that rope in the back of his truck to frame him."

"We found Dave by the trap. He had probably just put it there."

"But he wasn't carrying the trap when he went into the reservoir."

"It was dark, Rylie. You could have missed it."

I hadn't missed it. There was no trap.

"Look, we can arrest him on trespassing charges and take him down to the station for questioning. Then if he has an alibi, he'll be in the clear."

"And you'll take Patricia in for questioning too, right?"

"I have absolutely no evidence that she's involved. I'll try to set up another interview, but she already talked to us."

"She could be dangerous."

"She had every chance of offing you tonight and didn't, though it would serve you right if she had."

I wiped away the tears that had escaped my eyes when he wasn't looking. I didn't much like him thinking it would serve me right to be dead. We walked back to Dave's truck in silence.

I was more convinced with every step that Dave wasn't the killer. There was no way he would have been able to throw that cage with Ronnie's limp dead body into the reservoir by himself. He was bigger than Ronnie, but not by a lot.

"We found a pair of gloves with pieces of the rope embedded in the grips," Jerry said when he saw us.

"I didn' do it. There's no way I would have set those traps." Dave sat on the curb, hands still cuffed behind his back.

"Rylie may have found the murder weapon earlier

today." Luke held the plastic bag open for his partner to have a look.

"You touched it?" Jerry asked. "Please don't tell me you touched it. How stupid are you?"

"Careful, Jer," Luke warned. Why, I didn't know, since he had just said basically the same thing.

"I—I don't know. Maybe it wasn't—"

"I'll fill him in in the car," Luke interrupted, shooting a meaningful glance in Dave's direction. "Dave, you're under arrest for trespassing. You have the right to remain silent . . ."

He droned on reading Dave his rights as we all disbursed. Antonio, Shayla, and I walked back to where we'd parked our vehicles. "Where'd Kyle go?" I asked.

"He had to get home to the wife," Antonio said. "Fishing and family. Not much that's more important to that guy." He rolled his eyes at the last bit, and I wanted to punch him. Obviously, Kyle's talk hadn't gotten through to him after all.

8

"I don't buy it," Ben said the next day when I showed up for my practical test. "No offense, I know you're the one who caught the supposed killer, but I just don't think Dave could have done it. He might have been jealous of Ronnie's state record, but he'd have never killed him."

"I agree." I nodded.

"You do?"

"I do. There's something weird about the whole thing. It's almost as if someone planted the evidence against Dave. Someone who knew he'd be there."

I didn't want to give Ben my entire theory, but I'd tossed and turned all night over it. Now I was certain. It had to have been Patricia. She had mysteriously disappeared when the cops showed up and had probably planted the rope and gloves in the back of Dave's truck. If only I'd had my wits about me to ask her more questions.

"But who could have done that? The only people there were rangers and cops."

The only people he knew of.

I shrugged. "It could have been anyone. Dave's truck was parked completely out of view, a couple blocks away."

"I hear they haven't even interviewed all of the suspects yet."

He was right. I didn't want to cast any doubt on Luke's investigation, but they still hadn't found Clark—Ronnie's estranged fishing buddy—not that I thought he was the killer. And as far as I knew, they hadn't even questioned Jackson. Shouldn't they at least dot their *i*'s and cross their *t*'s?

"Either way, there's not much we can do about it. Today you're going to demonstrate all that you've learned in the past couple of days."

The practical test. My stomach dropped. This was my first chance to show, at least Ben, that I was the best choice for the full-time position.

"Where do we start?" I said with as much gumption as possible.

We started with a regular patrol. I drove while describing all of the rules and regulations I could remember and pointing out various landmarks. We pretended to use our radios, and Ben talked me through common scenarios.

After lunch, we took the boat out. It seemed as though all the progress I had made the day before had completely left me. I could barely pull up to a buoy without plowing it over no matter how many times I tried. It didn't help that there was a steady breeze. I was thoroughly flustered by the end, and Ben had to back the boat into the slip for me after a dozen failed attempts.

"We can't all be good at everything," Ben reassured me. "You'll get the hang of it eventually."

I highly doubted that.

We walked back up to the office to refill our water bottles and take a bathroom break when Carmen cornered me.

"Dave's innocent," she whispered. Her eyes darted around making sure no one overheard, even though Ben was in the bathroom and the office was empty.

"Okay, I think so too, but I don't have any way of proving—"

"I do." She wiped the sweat from her brow. "But if I tell you, can you promise not to say anything?"

My curiosity was in overdrive. "But if it'll clear his name . . ."

"You have to promise," she insisted.

"Okay, okay, I promise."

"I know he didn't kill Ronnie . . . because he was with me Sunday afternoon through, uh, Monday morning." She dropped her gaze to the floor. "No one can know, and I know he'd never tell anyone, not if he knew what was good for him, but I need you to keep investigating. I can help, just tell me how."

Whoa. Carmen and Dave. Carmen. Cute, well-endowed, *married* Carmen.

And Dave. Stinky, weasely, rotted-teeth Dave.

I'd seen it all now.

"I'm sure if we told the police, they'd keep your identity a secret," I said.

"No. No way. I have a reputation, and my marriage, to keep intact. And if it ever got out that I was sleeping with someone like Dave, I'd never hear the end of it."

She had a point. But then why sleep with him in the first place? Gross.

"I can keep looking and talk to Luke, but I can't promise anything. I'm not an investigator. I'm barely a passable summer park ranger."

She looked up at me. "From what I hear, you're a wonderful ranger. You already beat Nikki's record, and all the guys love you."

Sure they did. "Thanks."

"No, thank you. I don't want Dave to go to jail. It's not like it's love or anything, but I'd feel real bad, you know? If he was covering for me and took the fall for something like this."

I hoped she wouldn't let it get that far, but the look on her face said otherwise.

"Luke, I need to talk to you, tonight if possible. Call me back." I hit the red End button on my phone and tossed it in the passenger seat as I drove home. I'd apparently passed my practical test, because I was given a schedule with my name on it for the next week. Until then, I'd have two whole days off to investigate. But before I investigated, I was going to take a nice hot bubble bath and dive into one of the books that had been calling my name for months.

The house was quiet when I walked into the basement.

Mom and Dad likely weren't home from work yet, and Megan and the boys were in her apartment above the garage.

Fizzy flashed me his big puppy dog eyes that said, "I miss you." It had been a while since we'd been on a walk, and he was probably having people withdrawals sitting in this basement all the time.

"Okay, let's go," I said.

Fizzy ran around in circles a couple of times and then raced to where I kept his leash, grabbed it up in his mouth, and brought it back to me. He sat as still as a statue while I attached it to his collar and then he bolted toward the door, dragging me behind.

We walked at least three or four miles before my feet ached. When we got back to the house, an unfamiliar vehicle was in the driveway—a navy blue Ford Bronco. Probably one of my sister's friends. Her husband grew up in this town, and they knew everyone here. Either way, my slight curiosity wasn't going to get between me and my bubble bath.

My mom, however . . .

"Rylie, is that you?" She yelled down the stairs in her sweetest 'we have company' voice. Ugh.

"Yep, it's me."

"Will you come upstairs for a minute?"

I looked down at my running shorts and t-shirt. "Let me change and I'll be right up."

"Sounds good." And then she whispered, "And put on makeup too."

Heaven forbid I didn't look presentable enough for Megan's friends.

I changed into a pair of cut off shorts and a lacy white tank top, applied three coats of mascara and a bit of lip-gloss, and considered it the best I could do with such limited time.

When I came up the stairs, a man sat with his back to me at the table with my parents.

"Luke stopped by to say hi. Wasn't that sweet of him?" Mom said, her adoration of my high school sweetheart apparent.

I resisted the urge to shake my head. She had always been on team Luke, and here she was setting herself up for disappointment again.

Luke turned slowly in the chair, let his eyes travel over me, and beamed at me with his big flashy smile. It was a miracle that being in my parents' presence automatically took away his irritation with me. Faker.

"Great, I'm so glad you could stop by," I said through a smirk.

"He was just telling us about how the two of you have been working together on that murder case from this past weekend," Dad chimed in. "You didn't tell us you were working with *Luke*."

"It must have slipped my mind." I sat down at the table between Luke and Dad.

"Can you stay for dinner? I'm sure Megan would love to see you," Mom said.

"I actually wanted to see if Rylie wanted to join me for dinner tonight. To celebrate a recent break we've had in the case. That is, if you don't mind."

"You could have just called," I murmured.

"Don't be rude, Rylie," Mom chided. "Of course we

don't mind. Another time, though. You're always welcome."

"Thank you, Mrs. Cooper. I'll have to take you up on that."

My cheeks were starting to ache from the forced smile I wore. "I guess we'd better be going then."

"Dressed like that?" Mom looked at my bare legs and frayed shorts and then at Luke's khakis and button-down shirt.

"It's okay. We're not going anywhere fancy."

I fought the urge to stick my tongue out at my mom.

"I'll drive," Luke said when we were out of earshot of my parents.

"I can just follow you, then you don't have to drive me home afterward."

"Don't be ridiculous. Get in the truck." I heard the smile in his voice as he held the door open for me, something he'd always done when we were together.

I conceded and jumped up into the most pristine vehicle I'd seen outside a new car lot. Was I supposed to take my shoes off?

"This is nice," I said when he slid into the driver seat.

"It's all right." He shrugged and started the engine. "Sorry to show up out of nowhere."

"No, you're not."

"You're right, I'm not. You said you needed to see me, so I came as quickly as I could." He smirked. "Looks like your parents still love me."

"Of course they do. You were the 'perfect man' that I was too stupid to lock down. They're probably planning our wedding as we speak."

Luke let out a laugh.

"I take it you're not mad at me anymore?"

"I wasn't really mad at you, Ry. In fact, I should apologize. I was much harder on you than I should have been." He glanced over at me. "I just couldn't believe you'd put yourself, and Shayla, in that position. But Shayla explained that she had chosen to follow you against your direct orders—albeit rather stupid ones. Still, they helped us find the probable killer."

"Yeah, about that. Dave's not the killer."

"I know, I know. You think Patricia is, right?"

"Yeah, maybe. But I know for sure, one hundred million percent, that Dave is not."

"I know you like to see the best in people, Ry, but that evidence in his truck makes him the most likely suspect."

"In the *back* of his truck. Anyone could have put it there." I paused. "Plus I have a source—"

"You have a source?" Luke quirked an eyebrow at me and turned onto a small side street.

"Yes, I have a source, and that source told me Dave has an alibi."

"Then why wouldn't he have given us his alibi when he was interrogated?"

How could I give him the information without outing Carmen's relationship? "Um, well, probably because it's potentially . . . rather damaging."

"I'm pretty sure if I had an alibi, I'd tell the cops,

regardless how embarrassing. Especially when I'm facing murder charges."

He had a point. Apparently Carmen had Dave completely whipped.

"Just trust me. Dave's not the killer."

"Where does that leave us?"

I shrugged. "Clark? Or Jackson, maybe? Have you talked to either of them?"

"Not yet."

"Was there any DNA in the gloves you found?"

"Actually, now that you mention it, there wasn't."

"None?" I asked.

"Not a single trace."

"But if someone wore them to strangle Ronnie, wouldn't there be traces of skin left behind?"

"Maybe, maybe not," Luke said.

"Someone is trying to frame Dave. It's so obvious. You're the one who said I'm smart and observant. So listen to me."

"You're right, I did say that." He glanced over at me. "And I meant it."

He turned into the parking lot of a strip mall and shut off the truck.

"Pizza okay?"

The pizzeria was sandwiched between a massage place that probably offered happy endings and a bakery that displayed a yellowing wedding cake in its dust-covered window. Luke and his oddball places.

"See? You fit right in," he said once we were inside, motioning to a woman whose shirt was so sheer her nipples were practically saying hello. I jabbed him in the side with my elbow. "Sorry, I couldn't resist."

We sat in the back in a booth hidden from the door, and a waiter handed us each a menu. "Special tonight is the Caribbean pizza. Mango, pineapple, ham, and peppers."

"Ooh, that sounds good," I said.

"We'll take a large." Luke handed the waiter our menus. "Oh, and two Bud Lights from the tap. Hers with lime."

He remembered. Of course he did. My heart did a little flip-flop.

"Okay, so let's go over the suspects again."

"Can we talk about something else?" Luke's eyes pleaded. "Just for a little while?"

I shifted in my seat. "Sure . . . like what?"

"I want to know what you've been up to—from your mouth rather than everyone else's." He took a sip of the beer that had just been delivered.

I squeezed the lime into my glass and licked the excess juice from my fingers, my face puckering for the slightest moment. Luke shook his head and laughed under his breath.

"Well after graduation I went to Denver State and got my degree in parks and recreation. Then I moved back to the mountains and joined the fire department."

"And that's when you reconnected with Troy."

I took a gulp of my beer, letting the tart fizziness stream down the back of my throat. "Yep. And I worked for the town recreation department until all hell broke loose."

"How'd you find out he was cheating?"

"I caught him with Giraffe Girl in my—our—bed."

"Giraffe Girl?"

"It's what I called her. She was tall and had a super long neck." I shook my head trying to dislodge the mental image.

"I'm sorry, Ry. That must have sucked."

I nodded and took another drink of my beer. It had sucked.

We sat for a while in silence, each sipping our beers and watching the people around us. Well, he was watching the people around us. I was watching him.

The way he brought his glass to his mouth, holding it gently with the same swankiness he'd use on a fancy cup of tea. How he'd dab at the corners of his mouth with his napkin. Like a proper gentleman. His parents had succeeded in raising a good man. Though they'd always been immensely kind to me, I suspected they never quite thought I was good enough for their perfect boy. And he was definitely perfect. What was wrong with me? Why hadn't I just accepted his proposal?

Because I'm a self-sabotaging idiot, that's why. If I wasn't, I'd be this man's wife, the mother of his children.

"You okay?" he asked. I nearly fell out of my seat.

"Uh, yeah. I was just thinking about the case again."

Something in his eyes held mine for a moment, like he didn't quite believe me, but then he rubbed a hand through his hair. "Okay, go ahead. Let's talk about the case."

My mind reeled. What to ask, what to ask . . . "How do you propose we go about finding Clark?"

"No, no, no. There's no 'we' about finding Clark. I'm the investigator. I'll find Clark."

"But I want to help."

"You are helping. By keeping your eyes open and reporting back to me." The look on his face said the subject was closed for discussion.

"Thanks for dinner," I said as he turned into my parents' driveway and turned off his lights.

He jumped out of the truck and opened my door before I could get it myself. "I'll do some digging and find Clark. I'll also talk to Jackson."

"And maybe Patricia too?"

"And maybe Patricia too. Just please stick to keeping lookout. I don't need to worry about you while I'm trying to solve a murder."

I offered a non-committal shrug and a smile.

The stars were bright in the sky, and the moon lit our path to the basement entrance. "I guess I'll see you later then," I said when we reached the door.

The curve of his lips and the directness in his eye took me back to senior prom, the night he'd told me he loved me for the first time. My heart began to race.

"Rylie, I'm sorry I freaked you out in high school. If I had known how it would drive you away, I never would have—"

I put a finger up to his lips. "I was scared and stupid. I do wonder sometimes what life would have been like had I said yes."

His body radiated warmth, and I leaned into him just a bit. The electricity between us was palpable. My head urged me to take a step back, a deep breath, but it was as if our bodies were magnetized.

He leaned down and wrapped his arms around my waist. His mouth hovered inches from mine. I merely had to go the extra twenty percent. My heart raced and my arms moved without permission, circling his neck.

What would it be like to feel his gentle lips on mine again? I raised a fraction of an inch and could feel his breath when the porch light turned on.

Instinctively, as though I was still a teenager outside my parents' house past curfew, I pulled back.

After a moment of stunned silence, he burst out laughing. "You really need to get your own place."

9

"You were out late last night." Megan sat at the table with my mother drinking her coffee and thumbing through the leftovers of Dad's morning paper. All four boys sat in front of my parents' big screen TV watching some animated show with talking dogs.

"Luke and I were discussing the case." I poured myself a cup and joined them.

"It looked like you were *discussing* something very important when you were wrapped up in each other's arms on the porch." Megan glanced up from the paper, her perfectly sculpted eyebrows high on her forehead.

"You know, you could have asked him in," Mom said. "That's why you have full rein of the basement."

Sure, and she would have left us completely alone. Right.

I rolled my eyes and took the comic section. "We're just friends."

Megan shot Mom a sideways glance.

"Oh, stop it." We had to be just friends. That near-kiss would have launched us onto a completely different playing field. Was I even ready for that? It had only been a little more than a week since I'd left Troy.

"Penny for your thoughts?" Dad's deep voice startled me from behind.

"Nothing. Just thinking about the case."

"I thought you already caught the killer," Mom said, her voice an octave higher than normal.

"I want to make sure we caught the right guy, that's all."

"You always were one for justice." Dad kissed the top of my head. "It was nice seeing Luke last night."

Not him too.

"Did you have a good time at dinner?"

"Yeah, it was good." I peeked at my phone. "I'd better get going. I have a lot to do today." I had stayed up all night searching for information about Clark on the internet. I finally came across an address that wasn't far from the reservoir. What would it hurt to have a look around?

Clark's house was smack dab in the middle of the slums. With the windows dark and the weeds overtaking the lawn, it looked like no one had lived there for several months.

I circled the block a couple of times to make sure I knew the ins and outs of the area, then parked my car a few houses down, prayed no one would steal my rims while I was looking around, and walked down the crumbling sidewalk to his front door. If Clark was the killer, I needed to be careful, so instead of knocking I tiptoed around to the side of the house and looked through a window.

The sparsely furnished room had only a torn leather couch and a small tube TV on a metal folding TV tray. When I pushed, the window creaked open a hair. I cringed at the sound and waited, holding my breath. After a few seconds, I inhaled only to choke on the smell of stale pot smoke.

If they hadn't heard the creaking window, they definitely would have heard my coughs. But nothing moved inside the house.

The window was about waist high, and I looked down at my favorite pair of jeans and hoodie. Why hadn't I worn something I wouldn't mind getting dirty? Time to suck it up.

I pushed the window open a bit more and swung one leg over the window ledge, trying not to rip my severely tight pants. When I swung the other one over, I let out a breath. They hadn't torn. But when I stood up, I heard the dreaded sound of jean fibers ripping. I'd relaxed too soon.

The butt of my pants had caught on a stray nail in the windowsill. "Damn," I whispered. I reached back to feel at least three fingers' worth of bare skin where jeans should have been. Turning side-to-side, I tried to catch a glimpse of the tear. "Damn, damn, damn."

At this point I cared less about Clark finding me and cutting off my windpipe with a piece of rope than I did what kind of underwear I was wearing. A thong, of course. The rip, as far as I could surmise, was about three inches long and showed a good portion of my left butt cheek.

So much for my $180 pair of jeans. It'd take me months to save enough to buy another pair. Too bad patches weren't still in style.

"All right," I said loud enough for anyone in the house to hear. "If anyone is here, you better come out and face me. I'm not in the mood to come find you."

Nothing. Fine. Maybe that meant there was no one there. Maybe it meant someone was waiting to strangle me. Either way, my jeans were beyond repair.

I stomped from the small living room into the adjoining kitchen. On the table was an ashtray with several half-smoked joints and a moldy can of Spaghetti-O's with a fork sticking out the top.

My nose wrinkled with the smell. Nothing here.

I moved up the stairs that led to two bedrooms. One had a deflated air mattress and the other only had a futon with a saggy mattress. There were no clothes in the closets, no toothbrushes in the bathroom. Clark hadn't been here in a while.

My heartbeat went from a stampeding herd of buffalo to a dull thump. It was a dead end.

I made my way back down the steps.

A door squeaked open.

The stampeding herd was back. I grabbed the first thing I saw—the can of Spaghetti-O's—and held it up as a weapon. My mind drifted to the can of pepper spray sitting quietly in its holster in the trunk of my car. Great place for it.

The front door was completely open now—the sun streaming in through the living room to the kitchen—as I hid behind the wall separating the two rooms with the can raised high above my head.

Footsteps.

Slow, calculated.

He knew I was in here.

When the footsteps were just outside the opening to the kitchen I launched myself from behind the wall and threw the can where I expected there to be a head.

It made contact with the side of the man's face, spilling its vile contents all over his . . . uniform. Shit.

"Ma'am, you are under arrest." He grabbed my wrist.

"Under arrest?" I jerked my arm away. "For what?"

"Trespassing." The officer, likely the same age as my father, cuffed my hands behind my back as moldy Spaghetti-O's shook from his uniform and onto my hoodie. First the jeans, now the hoodie. Could this day get any worse?

The answer was yes.

When the officer walked me out to his squad car, a very amused-looking Luke leaned against the hood with another officer.

They were both struggling not to laugh.

"How did you know I was here?" I demanded.

"Did you not think we'd have surveillance outside one of the suspect's houses?"

Of course they would.

"That little dance of yours, though. What exactly were you celebrating? Getting inside through an already open window?" Luke teased.

"I wasn't celebrating." My temper flared. "I ripped my favorite jeans."

The two sets of eyes instantly traveled down my body. I turned and caught the older officer staring at the hole and nodding.

"Ahem?" I threw him the evil eye. "And now I have moldy Spaghetti-O's on my favorite hoodie."

"What about me?" The older officer asked. "At least you didn't get whacked in the side of the head."

Luke and his cackling buddy doubled over in laughter, shaking the patrol car underneath them.

I'd had enough. "Just take me in."

"We're not taking you anywhere." Luke grinned.

"Can you take off the cuffs then?"

He nodded, and the officer holding my hands behind my back unlocked my cuffs. I rolled my shoulders and rubbed my wrists.

"I thought I told you not to do anything that could put you in harm's way," Luke said, his voice only slightly more serious. He wasn't wearing a uniform like the other two. Instead, he wore jeans that hugged him in all the right places and a navy polo that looked like it might rip out in the arms if he flexed just right.

I shrugged. "I had a couple of days off."

He ran a hand through his brown hair. "Why are you so stubborn? Do I have to keep you with me at all times to keep you safe?"

My first thought was that I wasn't a china doll. My second was that it wouldn't be so bad to hang out with him all the time.

"I'm gonna go in and take a look around." The officer

next to Luke stood to his full height and walked inside while his partner cleaned the moldy goo from his chest.

"There's nothing in there," I shouted after him. The empty closets came to mind. "Other than a few half-smoked joints."

He didn't listen and Luke shook his head at the ground. After a few minutes of silence, the officer walked back out holding a note in his gloved hand.

"Look what I found in the freezer next to a bottle of vodka."

He held it out for Luke and me to read.

Ella, if you find this before I find you, I'll be in the mountains. Don't drink the booze. Come find me.
Love, Clark.

"And there was a business card with it." He handed Luke the card. "Looks like a motel."

"What're you doing the rest of the day?" Luke asked me.

"Really?" Excitement welling in my chest.

"Only so I can keep my eye on you."

"Let's go to the mountains."

"Feel better?" Luke asked when I'd changed into a pair of cheap jeans we picked up at Wal-Mart.

I removed my hoodie to reveal a plain white tank top. "Much. So what's the plan?"

"Well, I figure we can take a trip up to this motel and see what we find. Maybe we'll get lucky and Clark will still be there."

"I should probably text my mom and tell her I won't be home at a decent time tonight."

"If at all," Luke winked.

I might as well have melted right there in his front seat.

After an hour's worth of chatting about what Luke had been up to since graduation—working for the PD, not dating anyone seriously, getting a dog and a townhouse—the conversation seemed to circle back to the elephant in the room—the moment I broke his heart.

"All right, let's just talk about it," Luke finally said.

"Talk about what?" Maybe if I played dumb . . .

"About what happened at graduation."

Fine. "What do you want to talk about?"

"Well, I think it best we stop tiptoeing around it so we can move forward."

"Okay, you go first." I had practiced this moment in my mind since I'd seen him that night we found Ronnie's body, yet my thoughts were completely blank.

"You were my everything in high school. We were the 'it' couple, you know?"

I nodded.

"So I thought the only way to go was to get married. I mean, I knew we had different plans after graduation, but I assumed we could make it work." He raked his fingers through his hair. "I was a stupid kid. I still thought love would conquer all."

He had always been the dreamer, the optimist.

His gaze was trained on the road. "And then you said—"

"No," I whispered.

"No." His voice stabbed with emotion.

"And then I ran away to college." I looked out the window to the growing mountains in the distance.

"And wouldn't return my calls."

Oh, the phone calls. I had forgotten about the phone calls. So many messages, so many emotions. "You weren't the only stupid kid. I didn't know how to handle it. I thought a clean break would be better for both of us."

He nodded. "I see that now, but at the time, I was crushed. If it hadn't been for the police academy and Janine, Shayla's mom, I don't know that I would have ever pulled out of my funk."

I didn't know what to say. I didn't know a two-letter word could cause so much pain and agony.

"And then I heard you were dating Troy, which, to be honest, completely baffled me."

"He wasn't always such a jerk." Why was I defending him?

Luke raised an eyebrow. "Uh, yeah he was. Since elementary school."

"I guess I thought he'd change. I don't know."

"People change far less frequently than you'd imagine."

That's what I was afraid of. Had I really changed

enough to try and start something again with him? And so quickly after my life had been upended?

Luke took one hand off the wheel and gently scooped up mine from my knee. The brush of his thumb over my palm sent shivers down my spine until the familiar feeling of anxiety welled in my chest. "Luke, I don't know if we should . . ."

He let go of my hand. "I'm sorry, I thought after last night . . ." His voice trailed off.

"No, it's okay," I said too quickly. "It's just that I think we should focus on the case right now."

"You're right. Let's focus on the case."

"And then we can talk about this again another time." Yeah like when hell freezes over. I mentally slapped myself in the head. How could I be so committed to someone like Troy yet have such terrible anxiety when Luke got within ten feet of me?

We rode in silence the rest of the way.

———

Eventually the highway opened up into a valley between several large snow-capped mountains. The breathtaking sight made me yearn to be back in Big Mountain, lounging on the docks in my bikini with the mountains all around.

"This is the place." Luke pointed to a rundown peach-colored motel. Its roof was bowed from years of disrepair, its paint chipping, its windows broken and plastic taped over in places.

"Not exactly the Hilton."

He pulled his Bronco into a parking spot next to the door labeled "Office," and we both got out.

"Follow my lead," he said.

The young girl behind the desk smacked her gum and put down her phone when we walked in. "Welcome to the Least Western Motel. How can I help you?" Her tone was that of a bored teenager trying to make a buck.

"My sister and I are looking for our big brother, and we think he might be staying here." Luke smiled.

At the news that Luke was probably available, the girl's face went from bored to swoon in two point seven seconds. Luke's smile had that effect on women.

"I'm not really supposed to give that information out." She looked around the lobby. "My dad would kill me."

"Oh, your dad owns this place? Very cool."

"Yeah, it is pretty cool, I guess." She ate up his every word.

"I know it's not something you should do, but we really need to find him. You see, he could be in trouble and we need to make sure he's okay."

"It's just that our customers come here because they know we value their privacy. Maybe he doesn't want you to find him."

Luke frowned. "Okay, I understand. Thank you anyway." He turned away, and I followed suit. I couldn't believe we were just going to leave after we'd come all this way. And why hadn't he just flashed his badge and gotten it over with?

"What's your brother's name?" She asked when we'd nearly reached the door.

"Clark," Luke turned around and smiled. "Thank you so much."

The girl twirled her fine brown hair around a paint-chipped fingernail. "I don't see anyone here by the name of Clark." She looked at their paper registrar. "Could it be under a different name?"

Luke thought for a moment.

"Ella," I jumped in. "His girlfriend's name is Ella. They might have registered the room under her name."

"Ella, Ella," she ran a finger down the list again. "Yep, looks like Ella's the winner. Room 109. But don't tell anyone I told you." She smiled at Luke and he winked.

"It's our secret. Thanks."

We walked out of the office, and I jabbed Luke in the ribs.

"What?" He asked.

"She was, like, sixteen."

"So?"

"You could get arrested."

"For talking to her? I did nothing wrong."

"Except use your charm and seductive smile to get answers out of her."

"Whatever works," he looked at me sideways. "You think I have a seductive smile?"

I jabbed him in the ribs again.

The door to room 109 was just like all the others—dingy and probably covered in invisible germs. I silently wished for a pair of gloves.

Luke knocked.

"What are you going to say if Clark is here?" I asked.

"I'm going to ask him some questions, that's all. I

don't have jurisdiction here, so if I think there's something suspicious, I'll have to get the local authorities involved."

Luke knocked again.

"I don't think anyone's home." I tried to peek in the windows. "Wait, I think I see something."

Luke took my place. "Yep, those are legs."

Two skinny legs attached to a pair of cheap heels lay on the floor, the rest of the body obstructed from view by the bed.

Luke pounded harder on the door. The legs didn't move. He tried the handle.

Nothing.

"I'll go back and see if I can get a key." But before I could walk away, Luke lifted a leg and kicked the door in. "Or you can just kick it down, I guess."

"Flimsy motel doors," he muttered.

As soon as the door was open, a pungent aroma of dirty socks, urine, and something I couldn't quite put my finger on hit me—not that I would want to put my finger on or anywhere near a smell like that. The room was dusty and dark, clothes spread all over the floor and beds in a right mess.

Luke stepped inside, gun drawn.

"What is that smell?" I asked.

"Why don't you stay outside?" Luke said without looking at me. "We may need to call an ambulance . . . or a coroner." He said the last part under his breath, but I heard it just the same.

Those legs couldn't possibly belong to another dead body. This was not what I signed up for.

Luke cleared the bathroom first then made his way around the single queen-sized bed holding his flashlight to see in the dim light. His face turned from intense concentration to disgust in a split second.

"Ma'am?" He nudged the legs with the tip of his pristine Adidas shoe. "Ma'am?" He bent down and I followed. I didn't care what I was going to see. Being a firefighter hadn't been all sunshine and rainbows. I was a big girl, I could handle it, and maybe I could help.

The body of a limp girl—or woman, rather—lie in an odd position, face down with her arms and legs skewed all over the place. A pool of vomit intermingled with limp strands of blonde hair, now stained a putrid orange.

Luke rolled her over and checked for a pulse. Just as I was about to let out a breath, he nodded. "She's alive. Barely. Call an ambulance."

I gladly removed myself from the horrid scene and called 9-1-1.

———

"It looks as though she may have overdosed," Luke said once the ambulance had taken her away. "She may be another victim. I'd like to stay in town until she regains consciousness."

I nodded.

"If you want to get back, I can call you a cab, or you can take my truck and I can rent a car . . ."

I shook my head. "I'm off tomorrow, and I want to know what happened too."

Luke nodded. "Then let's find somewhere to stay."

"Preferably not this place." I gestured to the motel we were in, where visitors had returned to their rooms after playing looky-loo when the ambulance arrived.

"Couldn't even if we wanted to. There's some sort of convention in town, and it's completely booked."

What kind of convention? An illegal pharmaceutical convention?

At least this meant we'd get a better room than the one that girl nearly died in.

"I'll check around and see what's available, okay?" Luke asked.

I nodded.

I don't know whether it was unfortunate or fortunate that there was literally only one room left in the entire twenty-mile radius. My heart fluttered with the thought of spending a night in such close proximity to Luke, but then the rush of anxiety brought me back to my senses.

"Holy moly, this is our room?" I walked into a room that looked like Valentine's Day had thrown up at a New Year's Eve party. Long-stemmed red roses in crystal glasses graced tabletops, a bright pink down comforter lay across the king-sized bed, a glittery chandelier hung from the ceiling.

Luke's face matched the rosy red curtains. "It's all they had."

Champagne and chocolate covered strawberries sat on a silver rollaway cart near the bed. "What did you tell them?"

"They inferred. I—I didn't . . ."

His face made me dissolve into a fit of giggles. It felt

good to laugh around him again, to shake off some of the awkwardness from the truck.

I took a bite of one of the strawberries and savored the sweetness as its juice ran down the corner of my mouth. "Mmmmm, these are delicious." I held one out and he took a bite.

"Mmmm." His face softened as he gazed down at me. "They are good." He licked his lips, but bits of chocolate stuck to the corners.

"Here, you have something . . ."

I reached up to wipe the chocolate off with my thumb but he caught my hand in his. His eyes were pools of chocolate themselves, begging for the go-ahead. Before my anxiety could hit, I stood on tiptoe and pressed my lips against his.

At first, he hesitated, unsure, but within seconds his arms were wrapped around my waist, pulling me into him. His tongue eagerly met mine. It felt like being back in high school all over again, except different. He may not have dated anyone seriously, but he certainly had improved his technique.

I pulled him closer as his hands searched my back and up my sides. I wanted him, now, in this gaudy, overdone, excruciatingly beautiful room. I wanted to sink with him into the pink down comforter and feel his weight above me. I wanted—

"We can't." He pulled away, his eyes still closed as if he couldn't say no while still looking at me. My fingers hesitantly loosened their grip on his soft brown hair. "I'm sorry, I know you said—"

"I don't care what I said." I reached out for him again, but he took another step back, opening his eyes.

"Rylie, I really don't want to be your rebound . . . I can't be." He smoothed his hair down where my fingers had been. "We should probably head over to the hospital, and see if that woman's regained consciousness."

My heart was in my stomach. It served me right to feel the way I'd made him feel so many years ago. What was I thinking kissing him?

The ride to the hospital was uncomfortable to say the least. I didn't know whether to feel sad or mad, but I was pretty sure both were coursing through my body. Tears threatened to fall. I almost wished I were back at my parents' house. Almost.

On the way, he called one of his buddies from the academy and asked if he'd meet us at the hospital so we could talk to Ella.

The girl, who we confirmed to be Ella James, was still unconscious when we arrived. Luke and his cop friend went to speak with the doctors, giving me the opportunity to sneak into her room. I plopped down in a chair next to her bed and tried to focus on the case rather than my mixed up emotions.

Was I supposed to hold her hand? Talk to her?

No, that would be weird.

The nurses had cleaned her up nicely. Without puke in her hair, she actually didn't look so terrible. "What happened to you?" I whispered and leaned closer. And noticed the track marks up and down her arms.

The door of the room swung open, startling me so badly I almost fell out of my chair.

"Oh, thank God," I heard. The guy's voice sounded desperate. "I was so worried."

The man's eyes were focused directly on Ella as if I wasn't even in the room. He wrapped his arms around her floppy form and hugged her tight to his chest.

"Are you Clark?" I asked in a small voice.

He pivoted his head to look at me without letting Ella go. "Who's asking?"

"Uh, I'm, um," I tried to come up with a convincing lie, but my brain was frozen. "I'm a park ranger. Well, a seasonal park ranger. I mean, not forever hopefully, but—"

"Why is a park ranger in my girlfriend's hospital room?" He slowly lowered her to the bed and fixed her hair before focusing his full attention on me.

I wanted to call out for Luke, but I didn't want to spook Clark. I slowly stood.

"Your friend—Ronnie—he's . . ."

"Yeah, I know. What's it to ya?" He took a step toward me, and I took a step toward the door. Come on, Luke, come back, I silently urged.

"I found him. We—me and my friend—well, he's a cop—"

"The cops are here?" Ronnie's eyes widened before he lunged.

I ducked to the side before he could reach me, and when he yanked the door open, Luke was standing with his arms crossed over his chest.

"Leaving so soon?" Luke grabbed Clark by the shoulder.

Clark, a forty-something man wearing a superhero shirt identical to the one my youngest nephew wore nearly every day, stood only as tall as Luke's chest.

"My friend here has a few questions he'd like to ask you." Luke motioned to the uniformed officer behind him.

Clark's face went ashen. "I didn't do it. I swear."

"Why don't we go somewhere where we can talk?" Luke said.

"Do I need a lawyer?"

"You're not under arrest, but if you'd like a lawyer, we can take you down to the station and—"

"No, I'll talk to you." Clark's shoulders slumped.

Luke and I followed Clark and his officer friend down the hall and into the elevator to the first-floor cafeteria. "What were you doing in there? I turn my back for one second . . ."

He glanced over at me and I shrugged.

"I—I thought you already caught Ronnie's killer," Clark said when we found seats around a table that reminded me of the ones in our high school cafeteria.

"We have a few persons of interest, yes. But we'd like to know if you could give us any additional information about the circumstances surrounding his death," Luke said.

"Me and Ronnie, we've been friends for lots of years.

Always fishing together. 'Til he caught that damn catfish and started thinkin' he was better than everyone else."

Seriously, who cared about fishing that much?

"Can you tell us about the night he caught the catfish?"

"Sure," Clark shifted in his seat. "We were back in Muddy Water, usin' stink bait like always, and Ronnie gets a tug. Bigger'n any tug I ever saw. It took us both an hour to reel that sucker in, and by the time it was on shore, we knew it was close to the record.

"I didn' want Ronnie to take it to the rangers. I've had my bits of trouble with 'em in the past"—he looked at me apologetically—"but Ronnie talked me into it. So we loaded that big, slimy fish into the back of my truck and drove it around to the ranger station. I don' think the rangers much believed us though."

"What do you mean?"

"Well, they was asking a bunch of questions and makin' it sound like we was lyin' and such. Ronnie was too excited to notice, but they seemed irritated that we made them stay open late to take measurements and weights and pictures."

"Do you remember which rangers were on duty that night?"

Luke and I both knew Antonio and Kyle had been working.

"Oh I dunno their names, it was the Spanish one that all the girls like—"

Luke quirked an eyebrow at me.

"And the one with a permanent scowl on his face, looks like he needs an enema."

Yep, Antonio and Kyle, though I wasn't sure how he'd managed to mistake Italian for Spanish.

"And how did you know they weren't happy that they had to stay late?"

"Just a feelin', ya know? They was more irritable than usual, especially enema man—that's what we call him, not to his face o' course."

I stifled my internal laughter. The name suited Kyle.

"So then what happened?"

"Then—and this is the part that made me mad—Ronnie took all the credit for the fish. Like I hadn' even helped reel the bastard in. He said it was his rod, his bait, his fish. So I left him there."

Luke nodded.

"Can I go now? I need to check on Ella. She can't wake up without me bein' there."

"Speaking of Ella, what happened to her?" I asked, unable to control myself.

"What d'ya mean? She's just passed out, isn't she?"

Luke glanced at me sideways—a reminder that this was his interview, not mine. "We found her in your motel room lying in a puddle of her own vomit."

"I was at work all day. You can ask my boss. He's a good guy, gave me the job even with my history." Clark rubbed his wrists absentmindedly just like I had when I'd gotten the handcuffs removed that morning. "My last trip to the slammer woke me up, got me clean. But Ella, she's still working on it. I knew I shouldn'a left her by herself."

"Where were you the night of Ronnie's death?" Luke asked in a serious yet nonchalant voice.

"I was in the slammer. Down in Arizona. I figured you

already knew that." He looked from Luke to me, and back again. "When I left the reservoir that night, I wanted to get away. I was so mad, I drove all the way there, and when I got there—I admit—I drank too much. Got me locked up. I was in jail a week before they let me out. By that time, Ronnie was already dead." His eyes shimmered with tears. "I may have been mad at the guy, but I'm no killer. He was my best friend."

"If you were in jail, why didn't we find you in the database?"

"Ah." Clark smiled for the first time. "Because my name's not really Clark. It's Sue. My parents loved that stupid song."

Sue? Wow, poor guy.

Luke nodded. "I think that's all we have for now. But don't leave town in case we need to get in touch."

"I don't plan on it. Ella and me got a real good thing goin' on. I just hope this gets her to stop doin' those stupid drugs."

Luke's friend shook our hands and led Clark back upstairs, leaving the two of us sitting side by side, the awkward silence returning. To take my mind off of the incredibly sweet, handsome, and one hundred percent off-limits man sitting next to me, I thought about Ella. I hoped this was the wake-up call she needed. It wasn't every day a girl found a man who cared so much for her. I stole a glance at the man next to me and let out a sigh.

10

The once charmingly overdone room was now a sickly sweet torture chamber. Luke let me have the bed while he slept on the sofa. I texted my mother to tell her I wouldn't be home until the next day and ignored all of her follow-up questions. I didn't have the patience for her interrogation.

The next morning I rolled out of bed before Luke's tiny snores ceased and took a shower, hoping to wash off some of the stink and utter embarrassment that still clung to me from the night before.

Maybe he didn't have to be a rebound. Maybe I'd actually gotten over Troy faster than a normal person would.

But as much as I tried to convince myself that Luke and I stood a chance at a relationship, I knew deep down I wasn't ready.

That didn't make me want him any less, though.

After towel drying my hair and tugging on the same jeans and tank as the day before, I swiped some mascara over my lashes and deemed myself acceptable to face the day . . . and Luke.

But when I emerged from the room, Luke was nowhere to be found. Great, had he left without me? No, he was too good a guy for that.

I plopped down on the sofa where, just minutes before, he lay sleeping and picked up one of the pillows. I brought it up to my nose and inhaled. It smelled like his peppermint shampoo, the same kind he'd used in high school.

"What are you doing?" At the sound of Luke's voice, I practically threw the pillow on the floor in front of me. How had he gotten in without me hearing?

I'm sure my face was the color of the pink comforter that was haphazardly tossed on the bed where I'd slept. "I —I was—"

"I brought coffee." He held up two take-out cups. "And I confirmed with the Arizona authorities that Clark —or rather, Sue—was in jail when Ronnie was murdered."

"Damn," I said under my breath. "I'm sorry." Though I was secretly happy it hadn't been Clark.

"Don't be. It's good to rule him out." He handed me my coffee, and I took a sip of the aromatic black gold. "And today we have a meeting with Ronnie's wife."

"Patricia?"

"Yes, and she's agreed to talk to the both of us. She actually seemed rather excited to speak with you."

After our last rendezvous, I wasn't sure what to expect with her.

"About last night—" I began but he held up a hand.

"It's okay, I understand. There's always going to be chemistry there. You were my first everything."

"And you were mine," I said into my coffee.

"You can't blame yourself. We both had a part to play in it, but it's better that we're just friends. At least until things settle."

I knew what he was saying. Until I was certain I was over Troy. Dammit, how was Troy still controlling my life? Asshole.

"Agreed." Not really. Ugh.

"So are you liking the job?" Luke asked when we started back down the mountain toward the city.

"I am, though I don't know how well I really know the job yet. I hear homicides are a relatively abnormal occurrence."

"I'm sure once the case is solved things will settle down for you. And your co-workers, do you like them?"

I imagined Antonio and Shayla and smiled. "They're characters that's for sure."

Luke quirked an eyebrow at me. "Law enforcement types?"

"More like mall cop, but in a good way."

Luke let out a burst of laughter and a bit of the tension between us seemed to melt. "What do you mean by mall cop?"

"I don't know. Not so serious. More laid-back. No guns or handcuffs." Every word I said elicited more laughter. "What? Stop laughing." Now I was laughing too. "They're good people. I'm sure they're very good at what they do. And I'm one of them now."

"Oh you are?" His laughter died down, and he put on a mock serious face. "Forgive me Miss Mall-cop."

I swatted at his arm.

"Hey! Have you forgotten rule number seventeen?" His tone took me right back to high school and our flirtatious banter. "No hitting the driver."

"I'd barely call that a hit. More like a lo—"

His phone rang and my face felt like it would burn up. Thankfully, I hadn't finished the statement, but Luke's expression told me that he knew exactly what my next words were going to be—love tap.

"Hannah," he said bringing the phone up to his ear. After a series of *uh-huh*'s and *got it*'s, he said goodbye.

"What was that about?" I asked hoping he'd forget what had transpired before he'd gotten his phone call.

"That was Jerry. He spoke with Jackson today, and he has an air-tight alibi. There's no way he was the killer."

I figured as much. "Anything else?"

"Nope. That's about it." He didn't look at me when he said this but kept his eyes trained on the growing city out the windshield.

"You sure?"

"Yep. I'm sure."

I wanted to push it, but we were finally back on good terms and that meant more than whatever he was hiding. For now.

Patricia was on the front porch of her trailer house when we pulled up. She sat in a plastic lawn chair on the grass turf porch sipping what looked to be a Bloody Mary.

"It's abou' time you showed up." Her voice was slurred, and her eyes were bloodshot. They darted from me to the trailer across from us. "Let's go inside. The damn neighbors are always watchin' us . . . me."

Luke and I followed her inside the trailer and sat together on a couch that looked like it'd been upholstered in the seventies—yellow with brown and orange flowers, cigarette burns all over, and smelling of must and smoke.

She plopped into an armchair across from us. "So whaddya want?"

Luke looked at me. Apparently this was my interview.

"Well, uh," I cleared my throat. "I know you said you think Dave's the killer and all, but I'm not so sure."

"Dave did it, that bastard. He took my Ronniekins away from me." She forced out a dramatic sob and nearly spilled her drink down her front.

"How exactly do you know it was Dave?"

"Who else coulda done it? Dave hated Ronnie. After Ronnie caught that stupid fish, Dave was a bully. And Clark done runnoft."

Something about the way she said Clark's name set off my radar. "What exactly happened between Ronnie and Clark?"

"I dunno, stupid fishin' shit."

She looked away.

"You know, we saw Clark yesterday. He was very broken up about Ronnie's death."

She perked up. "Did he ask about me?"

148

"Well, no," I said and her face dropped.

"Not even to see how I's doin' without Ronnie?"

"He had other things on his mind," Luke offered with a shrug.

"The tramp. That's what was on his mind." Her face was turning purple. "If Ronnie hadn' been a complete asshole, Clark wouldn'ta left at all."

I circled back. "And where were you when Ronnie died?"

"You mean when that SOB murdered him?" She took a swig of her drink. "I already told him"—she jabbed a finger in Luke's direction—"I's just here in my house, doin' my nails."

"And you thought Ronnie was . . ."

"Fishin'."

I glanced over at Luke. "You told Officer Hannah you thought Ronnie was in the garage."

"Well, yeah, I did. I mean, I—I don't know—" she let out a sob that sounded like a pissed off cat. It took every part of me not to roll my eyes. Did she really think I would let this go because she cried? Luke shifted uncomfortably next to me. Typical guy, can't handle a girl crying. These tactics may have worked on Luke and his partner, but I knew a fake when I saw one.

"Patricia, do you like to fish?" I asked.

"I, well, I—" She blew her nose on a stained handkerchief she'd pulled from her bra. "I use ta like going with Ronnie and Clark. But when Clark left, it wasn' so fun anymore."

"What do you mean it wasn't fun anymore?"

Panic washed over her face.

"It's okay," I said in a softer voice. "We're just trying to find out who killed Ronnie."

She nodded and dabbed at her eyes. "It's just, Clark was a bit of a shield between me and Ronnie. When he was gone, me and Ronnie fought all the time."

"Did you and Clark ever spend time together when Ronnie wasn't around?" I asked. Luke shifted on the couch next to me.

"You can' possibly think . . . no." She shook her head violently. "We wasn' nothin'. I mean, I woulda been there for him, but he had that stupid little strung out bimbo from the slums he'd always run to."

Her voice cracked. So much for being *so* in love with her Ronniekins.

"So you were home painting your nails and Ronnie was fishing." I changed the subject.

"Yep. Apparently he didn' care that I didn' want him to go. Snuck out, he did." She looked at Luke. "I didn' wanna tell ya, because I didn' want ya to think I killed him."

"We're just trying to get all the facts, Mrs. Tilsdale," Luke said. "If there's anything else you left out in your first interview, please tell us. It may help us find Ronnie's killer more quickly." He flashed her the same smile he'd given the girl at the motel.

She blushed. "Well, don' take this the wrong way, but I followed Ronnie that night."

I shot Luke a sideways I-told-you-so glance.

"He went through that same gate I led you to. I sat in those bushes 'til it was dark. And the only person who came out those gates was Dave."

But Carmen said Dave was with her that whole evening. "Did you actually see Dave's face?"

"Well, no. But who else wears a stupid-ass full-body green onesie to fish? He's the only one out there I've ever seen wearing it, and I been out there a lot."

"A onesie? You mean waders?"

"Whatever they's called, he was wearing 'em, just like he does every time."

I had seen Dave twice, and neither time was he wearing waders. I had seen him in head-to-toe black though. "He wasn't wearing waders when he was taken to jail."

She shrugged. "Maybe they's too hot that night."

"So you saw Dave leave, but you never saw Ronnie leave?"

"I just figured he met someone out there and . . . and, well," she blew her nose again, "left with her. It wasn' until the nice officer came to my house the next day and told me that he was d-dead." The sobs were uncontrollable this time. "I didn' mean ta leave all those nasty messages on his phone. I's mad. I thought he was with a girlfriend. I's such an idiot."

"I think that's all we have, right, Rylie?" Luke stood from the couch.

No, that wasn't all. This lady was a first class liar. I didn't believe these tears in the least. But Luke wasn't making a suggestion.

"We'll let ourselves out."

I stood and walked out, glaring at his back the whole way.

"Why in the hell did you stop the interview?" I asked when we were securely within his truck.

"I think it's obvious, she didn't do it."

"What? Because she cried? She's a liar and a fake. And what was that about the messages she left on his phone? Did you know anything about that?"

Luke hesitated. "Yes. We obviously went through all of Ronnie's messages, and there were some rather threatening ones from Patricia."

"And you magically forgot to tell me about this?"

"It's an ongoing investigation. I can't tell you everything. I could get in a ton of trouble for what I've shared with you already."

"Really? What happened to you needing my help on the case? It was just a one-way street?"

"You already thought she was guilty. I didn't want to give you any additional ammo against her."

"She. Is. A. *Liar*. How can you not see that? Her tears weren't real. She told you one story and me another. Who knows, maybe she wanted him dead because he drove Clark away—the man she actually loves."

"You think she loves Clark?"

I fought the urge to physically slap myself on the forehead. "How dense can you be? Didn't you hear how she was talking about him? How everything wasn't fun after Clark was gone? How she despises Ella?"

Luke ran a hand through his hair. "Either way, I still don't think she killed him."

"She admitted she was there."

"And that she saw Dave leaving."

"She saw a man in waders leaving. I've never seen Dave in waders."

"Have you seen *anyone* wearing waders while fishing?"

Admittedly, I hadn't. But I hadn't worked there very long either.

"I think it's time you accept that Dave could really be the killer. Maybe your source is just trying to protect him." Luke peered over at me.

"Have there been any other leads at all? Anyone else?"

Luke shook his head. "I'd think you'd be happy we're narrowing it down."

But I had to find the real murderer, so Dave wouldn't go to prison to protect Carmen's honor.

My mother was not thrilled that I wouldn't answer her questions when I got home. After the tension-filled car ride with Luke, all I wanted was a bath and a book. Thankfully, the next morning I had to be to work early—the opening shift—so my mother didn't have a chance to corner me.

Ben was already at the shop when I arrived, coffee in hand. "Ready?"

"Yep."

"Any questions before you go on your way?"

It was my first day of being in one of the summie trucks, doing my own thing. "Not that I can think of. I'll call you if I need something though."

"Okay, you get the gates on the back fence line, and I'll get the main gate. Then we can meet in the office for coffee."

"Got it. Thanks."

The summie truck was much smaller than the full-time ranger trucks. It smelled like someone had left a tuna fish sandwich under the seat in the summer sun for an extended period of time. I felt like I should put down a plastic bag to make sure the stains in the seats didn't transfer to my pants but thought better of it. I couldn't get a name for being a priss.

The reservoir was still dark as the sun had yet to rise over the horizon. Headlights from the main gate indicated fishermen waiting for their opportunity to catch 'the big one' that would inevitably be impossible to catch in the heat of the day. Or so they claimed.

The path was completely void of bikers and walkers as I wound my way around to the smaller gates where they'd be entering in mere minutes. Everything was calm but the anxiety that welled within me. I took a deep breath and stepped out of the truck. I couldn't shake the feeling that a murderer lurked around every corner, waiting for me, ready to pounce the minute I opened one of the gates.

I squared my shoulders and put my fists on my hips in a superhero pose that Cosmo Online promised would make me feel brave. I didn't know how brave I'd feel if the murderer found me. You couldn't be brave if you were dead.

The hinges on the gate in Muddy Water Cove squeaked as the sun peeked over the horizon. Finally, some daylight. A tiny bit of my anxiety washed away until I heard a noise in the bushes where I'd once hidden.

"Is someone there?" I stepped toward the sound. "The park is open now, if you'd like to come in."

The rustling stopped. It was probably just a cat.

I turned back to the gate and came face to face, or

rather face to chest, with a tall gangly man. I let out a squeak.

"Easy there, it's only me." Kyle's face smirked down at me. "Didn't mean to scare you."

"Oh. Hey, Kyle." I took a step back, trying to stop my heart from breaking through my rib cage. "I heard something over in the bush and thought I'd investigate."

"You've been doing an awful lot of investigation lately. You know, we rangers usually don't have this much activity. I hope you don't get bored without an ongoing murder investigation."

I knew he was teasing me, but his tone was still the serious stick-up-his-butt tone that made me slightly uncomfortable. "So are you heading out to fish?"

"Yep." He held up a rod and tackle box.

"Well, I'll let you get on with it. I'm supposed to meet Ben in the plaza soon."

I walked back to my truck with him trailing slightly behind me. Of all the rangers, he was the least likely to be my friend. I knew that. But for some stupid reason, I wanted to impress him. He was in charge, after all.

When I got back to the plaza, Ben showed me how to check my inbox that had a grand total of two emails. One from Greg welcoming me to the team in the most grandfatherly way possible. And the other that went to all of the rangers from Ursula, announcing she'd be holding interviews today.

Wait, what?

I read it more carefully. Sure enough, she'd be here today to hold interviews for the full-time position. So much for notice.

"Looks like I'll have an interview today," I said to Ben when he returned to the office with more coffee.

"Yep, you and all the other summies. Wait, did you just find out?"

"Uh, well, I've been off for the last two days, and you just showed me how to check my work email so..."

"Don't worry, I'm sure Ursula will understand why you're in uniform."

Right. If I had known, I'd have probably added a change of clothes to my bag, complete with a dreaded pair of pantyhose. Ugh, maybe it was better that I hadn't known. At least now I wouldn't have to stuff my legs into those awful sausage casings. And she'd probably understand. I mean, I *was* doing the job I was hired to do.

By noon, Shayla, Brock, Nikki, and I all sat in the main office waiting for our chance to wow the Director. Shayla wore a slimming pair of pinstriped pants and a blouse with a sweater over top. She kept wiping the sweat from her face, and I had the urge to tell her to just remove the sweater, but I didn't want her to be any more nervous than she already was.

Brock was in a simple white button down and skinny tie while Nikki wore a crisp pencil skirt and jacket combo that made her look like Miss America just became the CEO of Google. My uniform looked frumpy and downright unprofessional compared to them. What did it matter anyway? Surely, they'd choose Nikki for the position.

Shayla went first and then Brock. Nikki and I sat in silence waiting our turns. When Nikki was called up, I said, "Good luck."

"I don't need luck. I have this in the bag." She pulled

her suit jacket down and strutted out like she was on a catwalk. Maybe I should just bow out now.

Nikki's interview seemed to take longer than the other two, and by the time I was called into the banquet hall, the interviewers looked irked that they had to do another interview when naturally they already knew who they were hiring. Or maybe I just thought that's the way they looked.

Five people stared back at me as I sat in a chair, nervously contemplating whether to cross my legs at the knees or the ankle. After introducing themselves as higher-ups in our department, Ursula began with the questions.

"If you were a bug, what kind of bug would you be?"

A bug? What the hell kind of question was that?

"Uh, well." I tried not to shift my weight. Bug, bug. What kind of bug? "A moth," I blurted out.

A moth? Really? I couldn't even come up with something like a butterfly?

"Why a moth?" Ursula asked in her best fake-nice voice.

Yeah, Rylie, why a moth? Ugh. I was so stupid. "Well, moths are, uh, resourceful, and kind of bland, but they're attracted to bright lights."

The panel made notes, looking as confused as I felt. Hopefully, that was just an icebreaker question.

"Okay, second question: Name five uses for a stapler, without staples."

For real? I could use it to bash myself over the head to get out of this interview. No, that's probably not what they were looking for.

Think. Think.

"Uh, you could use it for a door stopper to hold the door open. You could use it as a paperweight." That was only two. I needed three more. What else? Who cared how a stupid stapler could be used without staples?

"You could dismantle it and take the spring out to use in an emergency situation. Maybe it could be a musical instrument, like symbols only . . . clankier." Clankier is not a word. Get it together. "And last, it could be used as a hat."

"A hat?" Ursula spit out.

A hat? What the hell?

"Sure, I mean, you could put it on your head, that is, if you wanted to . . ."

Pretty sure Ursula rolled her closed eyes at that one.

"Let's move on."

Thank God.

"If we shrunk you to the size of a pencil and put you in a blender, how would you get out?"

Okay, this lady was nuts. Where did she get these questions and how did they possibly relate to being a ranger?

"Well, I'd probably dismantle the blades first just in case you wanted to turn the blender on." Which naturally, she probably would. "Then I'd shimmy my way up the sides, pop the clear circle thing out of the lid, and crawl out."

They all wrote down my answer, which I thought, for once, was pretty good.

"Okay, last one."

Only four questions? What about my strengths and weaknesses?

"If the park had 2,000 visitors and a storm was coming where you could only save 500 of them, how would you choose who gets to live?"

Holy crap. How was I, or any ranger, qualified to choose who lives or dies? Most people would probably say women and children, right? Or maybe they'd choose the doctors and teachers?

"I—I'm sorry. I can't make that decision."

"So you would just let them all die?" Ursula's bulldog face smooshed into an evil smile.

"No, of course not." What would I do? Think, Rylie, think. "Assuming, I as a ranger, can save 500 people, would it be fair to say that another ranger would be able to save another 500?"

Ursula looked up at me with her brow furrowed. "I suppose, yes."

"So I'd just need four rangers to save them all. And what kind of storm is coming?"

"Let's say a lightning storm."

Ooh lightning, that's a tricky one. It could come out of nowhere, or I could have time to prepare. "Well, in the summer, we staff at least two rangers at all times, and since lightning typically hits in the summer and in the afternoon in Colorado, we'd likely have at least three to four due to shift overlap. If we had four, we'd be able to save them all. If not, I'd call in the trail ranger to help."

"And how would you evacuate 2,000 people from the park?"

"Well, I wouldn't have to evacuate the park, necessarily. I'd just have to get people off the lake and in places where they couldn't get struck by lightning. So I'd send two rangers out on boats to warn the boaters before the storm came, and other and I would get people out from under trees, off the beach, and to the safety of their vehicles or inside a building."

They furiously scribbled in their notes.

"Thank you, Rylie."

They all shook my hand before I let myself out of the room. At least I didn't suck at the last question.

Shayla, Brock, and Nikki stood in a group in the plaza discussing their answers.

"Can you believe those questions?" Shayla asked when I walked in. "How'd you do?"

I shrugged. "Okay, I guess."

"Well, I rocked it," Nikki said inspecting her perfectly manicured nails. How did she keep them nice being a ranger?

"How did you answer the blender question?" Shayla asked.

"I said I'd punch through the damn glass," Brock said, his chest puffed out.

Nikki rolled her eyes. "If you were the size of a pencil, there's no way you'd be able to shatter glass that thick."

I wanted to ask how she'd answered, but at that moment Ursula walked out of the banquet hall with the rest of the panel behind her.

"We will deliberate and let you know our decision in a few days. Thank you all for coming." She looked at me and smiled what seemed to be a genuine smile. Maybe I'd done better than I thought. My heart leaped in my chest until I saw the murderous look on Nikki's face. Why did she have to be so mean? I turned and walked back to my truck. It wasn't like it was my call anyway. If they wanted to hire some wench like Nikki, they could deal with the attitude. I had a park to patrol. At least for the rest of the summer.

After walking the beach and shoreline for over an hour, checking on swimmers and fishermen, I decided to take one more patrol loop around the reservoir before I headed to the shop to clock out.

Opposite from the morning, now the bike path was completely packed with joggers and bikers, moms with strollers, and fishermen retiring for the day. Muddy Water Cove was completely empty. Apparently Kyle decided to pack it up before the sun hit its peak.

I glanced in the direction of where Ronnie's body had been found in the trap. The water was completely undisturbed. Maybe Ronnie had been the MWB and someone stuffed him inside his own trap.

Could it have been Dave? Was Carmen lying to protect him?

The part of me that had been so sure it wasn't him was now faltering. Everything pointed to Dave except my suspicions, that niggling little voice in the back of my mind. But there wasn't another trap, there wasn't any indication that the MWB had been back, and Dave was still sitting in a jail cell awaiting his time to see the judge.

When I circled back through the plaza on my way to the shop, the sight of Nikki talking to a very familiar figure almost made me drive straight into an oncoming car. And when I say talking, I mean flirting with every bit of effort in her body. She was touching his arm, giggling mercilessly, and flashing her great big model-esque smile. And Luke smiled right back at her like a big, stupid idiot.

I pulled into the ranger parking, threw the truck into park, and stomped over to them.

"Hi, Luke."

He spun around, surprised.

"Nikki." I crossed my arms over my chest.

Nikki glared.

"Hey, Rylie," Luke said as if him flirting with Nikki was a normal, everyday occurrence.

"Luke was just telling me about the case." Nikki reached out and squeezed his bicep. My hands clenched at my sides. If only it wasn't socially unacceptable to claw someone's eyes out.

"I thought the facts of the case were under lock and key," I said through gritted teeth. He wouldn't even tell me about Ronnie's phone messages, he'd hidden something from me on our drive back from the mountains, and here he was spewing all the details to some bimbo because she smiled at him. Some investigator he was.

Luke looked annoyed. "I was actually here to talk to you. But then I saw Nikki and—"

"It had been so long, we had to catch up."

Who was she to finish his sentences? And what did she mean it had been so long? They knew each other?

"Well, here I am. What's up?" Every part of me wanted to go back to my truck and peel out leaving them to make a baby right there in the middle of the plaza. What did I care? We *were* just friends after all.

"The judge let Dave out on bail today. I want you to be

careful in case he is the murderer. He's not supposed to be around here, so if you see him, call me. Do not rush in by yourself like you usually do."

Nikki covered her hand with her mouth in an overstated giggle at my expense.

"Got it," I said. "If that's all, I have to go." I couldn't stand there and watch him flirt with Nikki. It hurt too much.

He nodded, and before he could say anything else, I left.

1 2

Luke sent me a couple of texts that afternoon and evening, making sure we were on good footing. I finally responded that I didn't care who he flirted with—it wasn't like we were together—before falling into a mess of tears hugging Fizzy. At least *he* understood me.

Mom knocked on my door around six. "Dinner's ready, sweetie."

"Mom, I don't feel—"

"Oh, please come to dinner. I promise I won't ask anything about Luke." She used the voice that made me cry even harder when I was little, the one that said: "Mommy's here, I'll hug you and pet your hair and listen without judgment." And as a child, I believed her, but now I was wise to her tactics.

"You promise? No talk about Luke at all?"

"I promise."

I wiped the dried tears from my cheeks and squeezed Fizzy one last time. "Okay, I'll be up in a minute."

Megan and the boys sat nicely at the table while my dad and Tom sat in the living room watching golf. My mom busied herself in the kitchen adding the final touches on dinner before hauling two piping casserole dishes of cheesy goodness to the table.

When I was about halfway done and up to my elbows in some delicious mixture of cheese and noodles and chicken, Megan blurted out. "Why does it look like you've been crying all afternoon?"

I looked up at my mother who shrugged. "I didn't say we wouldn't talk to you at all, just not about Luke."

"Oh, you're crying over Luke?" Megan spooned a bite of casserole into her youngest son's mouth. "I guess it's about time the tables were turned."

"What's that supposed to mean?" I nearly spat out the partially chewed wad of food in my mouth.

"He was obviously distraught when you dismissed him so blatantly at graduation. Maybe what goes around comes around."

"And maybe I'm not crying over Luke." My temper was rising. I knew dinner was a bad idea.

"Okay, then why are you crying?" Megan pushed. She may be a mother, but sometimes she acted like we were teenagers fighting over who got to wear a favorite hoodie.

"I just had a bad day."

Mom reached over and patted my arm. "Did someone fish without a license?"

"No. No one fished without a license. Why would I cry about someone fishing without a license?" I stood up and threw my napkin on the table. "I'm so sick of being trapped in this house."

"Rylie, please lower your voice," Dad said. "And apologize to your mother."

My mother's eyes were wet as she dabbed at them with her napkin. My eyes flooded with tears.

Anger, shame, frustration.

I should have sat back down, should have apologized, but my pride wouldn't let me. Instead, I stormed out of the house and took off in Cherry Anne.

After driving long enough for my tears to stop, I found myself back at the gate where Dave had been arrested, the one that led to the scene of Ronnie's murder. Ugh. Why was this so important to me? I was an idiot to go back to the scene of the crime when Dave was out on bail.

I yanked the wheel to make a U-turn but before I was completely around, I hit the brakes and my car skidded to a stop.

Who was that?

A man dressed in what looked like the exact description Patricia had given was climbing over the fence. My pulse quickened.

I pulled out my phone and sent a quick message to Luke.

I'm at the reservoir. Someone's breaking in.

Within seconds he replied.

Wait for me to get there. Don't. Do. Anything.

I shoved the phone into my pocket and pulled the flashlight and pepper spray from my ranger belt. I couldn't wait for Luke. I had to catch Dave—or whoever it was—in the act.

13

By the time I reached the gate, the guy was long gone. Thankfully, I knew where he was headed, that is, if he really was the MWB. I hoisted myself over the five-foot fence and landed with a soft thud. My stealth skills needed work.

My eyes had adjusted to the darkness, and the moon let off a faint glow allowing easy navigation of the concrete path. The distance from the gate to the cove was only about a quarter mile, but it seemed to take an eternity to get there.

With my pepper spray in one hand, finger close over the trigger, and my flashlight in the other, I was ready for someone to jump out at me at any moment. I felt like a badass.

The cove was completely still except the water, where a cage had obviously been thrown. The swirling ripples made my heart jump.

I inched closer to the shoreline, keeping my footsteps as quiet as possible.

What if there was another body in the trap? There's no way I'd be able to hoist it onto shore empty, let alone with someone in it.

And where was Trespasser Guy? I saw him jump the fence, but maybe he went a different direction. Maybe he had traps placed elsewhere too. I took another step toward the shoreline and clicked on my flashlight to get a better look at the water, hoping the murderer wasn't waiting to jump out at me.

There was no denying it. A trap was definitely beneath the surface. Now, to find the rope. I may not have the strength, but I had to try.

I let my flashlight travel the shoreline ahead of me, scanning the brush for any signs of an anchor point, but before I could find anything, the sound of footsteps came from behind me. I clicked off the light and crouched behind a bush holding the pepper spray out.

The footsteps drew closer. Was it the murderer? What would he do if he found me here? I had to do something.

I reached for my phone and tried to wiggle it out of my jeans pocket. It was lodged in there. I extended one leg, trying to be as silent as possible, and finally my phone came free. But when I clicked on the power, a hand grabbed my shoulder.

"Gotcha."

My whole body flailed. I took an accidental step backwards, my foot landing in the water, my butt following, and my phone flying into the reservoir with a kerplunk. At least I still had the pepper spray in my hand. I aimed. "Don't come any closer."

"Rylie?" A flashlight clicked on and shone directly in my eyes.

"I'll do it . . ."

The light clicked off, and little orbs floated in my vision.

"Take my hand." The voice sounded more and more familiar.

"I can't see. You blinded me."

A hand reached down, grabbed me by the collar of my jacket, and yanked me to my feet.

"Kyle?" I said when I could finally see his face. "What are you doing here?"

"The same thing I assume you're doing . . . looking for the MWB."

"Well, he's here. He's wearing green waders. And he put out another trap."

Kyle threw me an irritated glance. "I've been observing this cove for hours, and the only person I've seen out here is you."

"Maybe he went another way, to set another trap."

"Or maybe you're the MWB." Kyle's patience seemed to be running out.

"You can't possibly think—how would I—" No, he couldn't think I was the MWB.

"You're here after hours, threatening to spray an officer of the law—your supervisor—with pepper spray."

Supervisor, okay. But officer of the law? That was a bit of a stretch. "I thought you were him. I thought you were the killer."

"Me? The killer?" His face was turning red. "You should go home. Summies have gotten fired for less than this."

"You're going to get me fired?"

He got closer to my face, definitely invading my personal bubble. "I'm your supervisor. I don't get you fired. I do the firing. Now go." He pointed off into the distance toward the gate.

"But the MWB, there's a trap just there." I pointed to where the water rippled.

"I'll check it out, but if I were you, I'd hope there was no trap, because if there was, I only see one person who might be guilty of setting a trap there. The only person here who knows *exactly* where it is . . ."

"It's in the same place we found the others. That's the only reason I—"

"Let's go." He grabbed my arm, hard, and pushed me back to the trail.

My chest felt like it might explode. How dare he think *I* was the MWB, let alone the murderer? How dare he put his hands on me? How dare he threaten to fire me?

I needed this job. I was just trying to help, and he wasn't even taking me seriously.

The murderer was trespassing right now, probably laughing at us from behind a tree, and this idiot was acting like I was the bad guy. Maybe I should have words with *his* supervisor.

Greg.

Ugh, Greg would never fire anyone. He was too nice. And it wasn't like I had an in with Ursula like Nikki.

I yanked my arm from his grasp and rubbed my bicep where I was sure a bruise would blossom by morning.

"Go home. Leave now and I'll drop it." He glared at me.

"Fine." I turned and walked back to my car. I sat there for a while, waiting for the trespasser to reappear, but he never did. Meanwhile an irritated-looking Luke showed up and reamed me for not answering his phone calls.

"I dropped my phone in the reservoir," I said.

"You weren't supposed to go in without me. You could have gotten yourself killed."

"It doesn't matter anyway. I probably won't have a job tomorrow."

"What do you mean?"

"Kyle thinks I'm the MWB. He threatened to fire me."

"That's ridiculous. Maybe I should go in there and—"

"No, don't," I panicked. "He said he'd drop it if I didn't tell anyone."

Luke frowned. "Maybe I should go in there anyway. Look around. Try to find the trespasser."

"He's long gone by now. Probably picked up and left when he saw Kyle and me arguing."

Luke's radio lit up, and I knew by the look on his face that he'd been called over his earpiece. "I have to go. Please, go home. And stop getting into trouble."

I nodded.

"And get another phone."

My legs were chafed almost as badly as my ego by the

time I snuck back into my house. Thankfully, my parents hadn't changed the locks on me since I'd been gone. Though I wouldn't have faulted them if they had.

How had I gone from on top of the world one day to screwing everything up the next? I had to make it up to all of them, somehow. I had to apologize to Mom, keep my job, and find the real murderer. Should be a breeze.

14

Mom wasn't awake when I left for my shift, but I left her a note of apology next to the coffee pot where I knew she couldn't miss it. Not ideal, but it was something.

Ben and Kyle were both at the shop when I arrived, having what looked to be quite a heated discussion. Great. Had Kyle changed his mind and decided to fire me anyway? At least it seemed like Ben was trying to stand up for me.

"Hi," I said in a meek voice when I walked over to them, but they acted like they didn't even know I was there.

"You shouldn't be doing night patrols without anyone else's knowledge," Ben said, his voice more irritated than I'd ever heard.

"Last time I checked, my badge had the number two and yours had the number four. You don't have the authority to question me."

"Did you find the trap?" I asked. The heads of both men turned slowly to look at me, as if I had magically appeared out of thin air.

"There was no trap," Kyle said through gritted teeth. "And I thought we were going to drop it."

Shit.

"So something *did* happen last night?" Ben turned his attention back to Kyle.

Shit.

"Nothing important. Rylie thought she saw someone break into the reservoir. Thought she saw a trap." His tone mimicked my high-pitched voice only with added annoyingness.

"I did," I insisted. "I was driving around and saw some guy in waders climb over the fence in Muddy Water Cove."

"Climbing that fence in waders would be nearly impossible," Kyle said. "But since you brought it up, I may as well let Ben in on my thoughts that you could be the MWB."

"That's not possible. I wasn't even here when the traps started showing up." I looked at Ben, pleading for him to believe me. "I was only out there to catch the killer. And when I got down to the shoreline, there was a trap. The water was swirling just like it had when we found the trap, Ben."

Ben eyed me with a skeptical look on his face. If he didn't believe me, no one would.

"So did you find it?" Ben finally asked Kyle.

"There was nothing there."

"Did you even look?" I asked, my tone becoming more frantic. "What if there was another body?"

"Why don't we all go back there now and see?" Ben suggested. "Though I'm not sure if it's in your best interest that we find one, kiddo."

"I don't have time for this. I've been patrolling all night. Freaking office politics. One little dead guy and everybody's got their panties in a knot. The two of you can go do your little investigatory work. I'm going home. I'm ready to see my wife." Kyle turned to leave then turned back. "I'm keeping my eye on you. One more misstep and you'll be asked to turn in your badge."

Panic welled inside me. Staying out of trouble was not my forte.

Ben looked like he was going to stop Kyle but then decided against it. When Kyle had driven off in his personal truck, we each took one of the ranger trucks and headed back to Muddy Water Cove.

I knew before we had even gotten out of our trucks. There was no trap beneath the waters. I didn't know whether to be frustrated or relieved. Had I been seeing things the night before? Or maybe the MWB had been back since Kyle's last circle around the reservoir to remove the trap.

"Looks like there's nothing there." Ben shrugged. "Probably for the best so Kyle can't try to pin it on you. What'd you do to make him hate you so much?"

"I don't know, but I do know what I saw last night. A

guy in green waders jumped the fence. And there was a trap."

"I hate to break it to you, but guys jump the fence all the time to get a better shot at the big one. It's not like the reservoir is Fort Knox. That's why we sometimes have overnight patrols, like what Kyle did last night."

"But he didn't tell anyone about it."

"It wasn't on the schedule, no, but Greg probably knew. And that's the only person he has to tell since he *is* Ranger Two."

"Do summies ever get to do overnight patrols?" I urged him to say yes. I needed this. I needed my chance to catch the murderer in action and prove my innocence.

"Well . . ." he rocked back on his heels studying me. "If a full-time ranger were there to assist in your learning, then possibly . . ."

"Great!" I would have jumped for joy if it wasn't for the eighty-pound boots on my feet. "How about tonight?"

"Tonight? You'll be hard-pressed to find someone to sign up for tonight."

"Can we at least put it out there?"

He ran a hand through his hair. "Sure. I'll send out an email and see what we get."

Within five minutes of Ben sending that email, both Antonio and Kyle responded that they'd be there.

"Who would you rather work with tonight?" Ben asked.

I didn't really love my options. My choices boiled down to the guy who wanted me fired and thought I was a criminal or the married guy whose physique made me feel like a hormonal teenager. Either way, I'd have to do my best to avoid them if I was going to catch the killer.

"Never mind. Looks like you don't have a choice. Kyle pulled rank. I guess he wasn't joking about keeping an eye on you."

Carmen stood when I walked into the main office. "Have you found the killer?"

I looked around to make sure no one was listening. "Carmen, are you absolutely certain that Dave was with you the night Ronnie was murdered?"

"Absolutely, one hundred percent."

"Then could you please talk to Luke about Dave's alibi? He promised to keep it confidential."

She shook her head so hard, I thought her gum might fly out of her mouth. "Nope, no way. I know what they mean when they say *confidential*." She air quoted the last word, flashing her pink sparkly fingernails. "They mean, they will only tell the people who need to know. Which in cop-speak means everyone."

She had a point. Cops did like to gossip, even if only between themselves.

"And if my husband ever finds out that Dave is my lover—"

Dave and lover in the same sentence? Gag me.

"He'd divorce me and leave me with nothing. He'd take my car and my house and probably even my . . ." She looked down at the cleavage that peeked out from her shirt. "No, he can't take these." She crossed her arms over her apparently unnaturally large breasts.

"Okay, all right. I understand."

15

The brief respite I had between my morning shift and overnight shift was filled with attempting to apologize to my mother and her shooing me away, acting as if nothing happened. Classic avoider. She'd mope and hold a grudge until she was damn well ready to forgive me, and there was nothing I could do about it. But I had to try.

When she decided she absolutely had to make her second trip to the grocery store for the day, I retreated to my room and took a nap with Fizzy. I woke up in a haze, my brain not fully realizing why I was forcing myself out of bed long before the sun came back up.

I put my uniform back on and prayed that my mother had left me a plate of dinner in the refrigerator. She hadn't. I guess she was madder than I'd thought.

I slunk out of the house and drove as quickly as I could to the phone shop to pick up a new phone—there went my first paycheck—before hitting up the local McDonalds for a burger and fries. I pulled into the reservoir just as Nikki was closing the gates.

"We're closed," she snarled into my partially open window. "Oh, it's you."

"Yep, I'm here for the overnight shift with Kyle."

"Good luck with that. If you thought he was a peach in the daytime, just wait until he's bored and tired."

The smile on her face made me cringe. "I think I can manage."

"Did you hear?" she asked, her smile turning into an evil grin.

"Hear what?"

"That I got the full-time position?"

My heart sank. It wasn't as if I really thought I would get it, but the way Ursula had smiled at me . . . oh well.

"Congratulations," I said with as much peppiness in my voice as I could muster.

Her smile drooped a bit. Kill 'em with kindness, my dad always said.

"Oh, and Luke is taking me out tonight so we can celebrate and catch up. It was *so* good to see him again."

Tears burned in the corners of my eyes, but I would not let her think she was winning. I blinked.

"Have a great time." I put Cherry Anne in gear as I muttered, "wench."

Once at the shop, I swiped the tears from my cheeks and took several deep breaths before I stepped out of my car.

Kyle and Antonio stood with two women, presumably their wives. On top of everything else, I really wasn't ready to meet the woman Antonio claimed to detest.

"Hi," I said with a small wave to the four of them.

Kyle's wife was his exact opposite. Short and bubbly. She shook my hand with a megawatt smile and more energy than a child hopped up on caffeine and sugar.

Antonio kept an obvious distance from his wife. She was tall and slender, with the body of a supermodel and the face of a horse. She didn't smile.

"So you're the new one, huh?" She glanced from me to Antonio with an ugly look in her eye. I just nodded.

Kyle's wife shifted from one foot to another. She leaned toward Antonio's wife. "We should probably be going. It would be unfavorable for the hosts to be late." She winked.

"Oh yeah, there's another game on tonight, right?" I did my best to smile. "The Avs look pretty good this season."

"It's just a shame Kyle has to miss another game." His wife pouted. "Between work and the flu, this poor guy just can't get a break."

"The flu?" I hadn't heard about Kyle getting the flu.

"Oh yeah, he had to leave the party early last game because he didn't feel well. Then tonight he got stuck with the overnight shift again."

Ummm, pretty sure he volunteered for the overnight shift. In fact, so had Antonio, even though he'd had a party to host. What were they playing at?

"It's all right," Kyle shrugged. "It's good money, and I don't like hockey nearly as much as I like football."

"I didn't know you were sick," Antonio said, his face a mixture of emotion.

"Just a twenty-four-hour thing. Nothing major," Kyle replied.

"Let's go already," Antonio's wife grabbed him by the arm. "We can't be late to our own party."

Antonio peeled his gaze from Kyle's face and studied me. Something wasn't right. Did Antonio know something? Did Kyle?

"Maybe I should stay and help you two out," Antonio said, pulling his arm from his wife's grasp. "I mean, there is a killer on the loose." He said the last part with his breezy Italian accent cranked up.

Some weird part of me was screaming, "Yes! Stay!"

"You can't be seriously considering blowing off all of your friends and your *wife*," his wife's voice was growing shriller, "to stay back and, and . . . work!"

Antonio shot her a glare, but Kyle cut in.

"It's really okay. I was here last night and nothing happened." He glanced at me. "Nothing important. I'm sure we'll be just fine."

"Rylie?" Antonio asked, obviously not caring what his wife or Kyle thought.

"It's okay. We'll be fine."

"If you're sure."

"She said they'll be fine," Antonio's wife hissed. Kyle's wife wrapped an arm around her shoulder.

Antonio offered a short nod. "Okay. But call if you need anything."

This was the last straw. His wife let out a frustrated yelp and stomped off to her car.

"It was nice meeting you, Rylie." Kyle's wife smiled. "And I'll see you tomorrow." She patted Kyle on the arm, her smile melting away, and then followed after her friend.

Antonio hesitated for a moment longer and then said his goodbyes before turning and following his wife. My gut told me to follow him. That tonight was going to go badly. But if Dave wasn't the killer, I needed to find out who was.

"So, do we share a truck or take our own trucks?" I asked when the other three had driven away.

"We have to share, so I can show you the ropes. Overnight shift is different." He turned on his heel and huffed over to his truck. "Get in, and don't get any dirt in my truck."

By hour three, I could tell Kyle thought the whole business of an overnight shift to find the murderer was pointless. He kept throwing in comments like, "How stupid were they to let Dave out when they know full well he did it?" and "Maybe the *real* cops should be taking these overnight shifts." I was ready to pull all of my hair out. No one forced him to volunteer to work. And he was the one who chose to work two night shifts in a row.

"Maybe we should split up," I said after his last comment. "I mean, I think you've shown me what I need to know, and if we both had eyes on the park maybe we'd find something—"

"Fine, I'll drop you at the shop, and you can pick up the summie truck. Just don't drive the boat."

I nodded. There was no way I was getting near that

thing, especially in the dark. With my luck, I'd end up sinking it faster than a dinghy in a hurricane.

When I was finally in my own truck, a tightness in my chest released. It was like I had been suffocating in Kyle's presence. Ben's training style was more my speed—patient and chill rather than micromanaging and negative.

My mind rushed back to Ronnie and his own suffocation. What a terrible way to die. Why would anyone want to kill him? I mean, yeah, he was kinda gross and annoying, but he wasn't much different than the other fishermen. Well, other than he had outdone them with his record catch.

My new phone buzzed in my pocket. A text from Luke.

Did you get a new phone?

I rolled my eyes. What did he care? He was probably out with Nikki at this very moment.

Yep.

The little bubbles showed he was typing and then:

Good. Working overnight, I hear?

How'd you hear that?

Nikki told me.

Nikki. Ugh.

Let me know if you need backup.

I shoved my phone in my pocket and stomped on the accelerator. I didn't need his backup.

I circled back to Muddy Water Cove and waited. And waited and waited. Two hours passed without a single hint of an intruder. How likely was it that the killer would sneak in two nights in a row? How stupid was I to think I could outsmart a murderer?

My phone buzzed, and I ignored it for the umpteenth time. I had no patience for Luke's crap right now. I didn't have time to dwell on it, though, because at that very moment, I caught sight of a man in waders walking down the shoreline.

"Ranger Fourteen, Ranger Two?" I called over the radio.

No response.

"Ranger Fourteen, Ranger Two?" I called again. The man disappeared behind a cluster of trees.

"Ranger Two, go ahead." He sounded as if he had been sleeping and I'd woken him.

"I have an intruder in the back of Muddy Water Cove."

"Okay, don't move until I get there."

Don't move? But he could be getting away. Again.

I sat still as long as I could, my eyes focused on the cluster of trees where the man had disappeared.

I almost texted Luke about the intruder. But my pride kept my phone firmly in my pocket. Plus, who was I to ruin his date?

We were friends . . . just friends.

At this hour he was probably home and asleep,

anyway. Though if he wasn't that would mean . . . no. Stop it.

My heart pounded. The thought of him with Nikki—kissing her, holding her—sent shivers of jealousy down my spine. I had to get my mind off them.

Where was Kyle anyway? My patience had run out. He was taking way too long to get here. It was almost as if he didn't want to catch the killer at all. Was that what he was hiding? Did he know the killer?

I had to act.

The shoreline where the man had disappeared into the trees was only about fifty yards from where my truck was parked. My boots were nearly silent and my breath was steady. I was going to catch him this time.

Fresh footprints lined the edge of the trees, defined by the softness of the mud. Good, the added mud on the soles of his boots would likely slow him down.

The moon was barely visible and provided little light, but my eyes had adjusted. I stepped into the trees. My pulse pounded in my ears as I listened for any sign of another human presence.

The leaves rustled in the wind, causing me to flinch but thankfully not make any noise. I stepped further in, removed my pepper spray from my belt, and held it at the ready. I couldn't wait to spray this asshole.

"Ranger Two, Ranger Fourteen?" Shit, I'd forgotten to turn down my radio.

The crunching of twigs and branches came from directly in front of me. He was running. I took off after him.

"Ranger Two, Ranger Fourteen, where are you?" Kyle

sounded pissed, but I didn't have time to respond. I sprinted through the trees lining the shore until I emerged and nearly ran right into the water.

Wait, where had he gone? I looked left and right. Nothing.

Had he gone into the water? No, the water was still smooth as glass. Maybe he'd doubled back.

I turned and ran straight into a man. I didn't even think. I just sprayed for his face.

"What the hell?" The minute I heard his voice, I knew.

Kyle.

Shit.

I put the pepper spray back.

"Why the hell did you spray me?"

"I—I thought you were—"

"What? The MWB? You are the biggest idiot I've ever come into contact with." He rubbed furiously at his eyes.

"Don't rub. It'll only make it worse."

"Get in the truck and meet me back at the shop. You're finished as a ranger."

Done? No. I couldn't be.

"But there's someone here."

"There's someone here," he mocked me. "This is the second time you've been wrong. The second time you've made a fool of yourself. And the last time you'll ever wear that badge again."

No. He couldn't fire me. Okay, so maybe I'd attacked him, but in my defense, I didn't know it was him. I thought he was a murderer.

"Please, just hear me—"

"Shop. Now." He turned on his heel.

Tears threatened to pour from my eyes. The drive back to the shop was both too long and too short. Kyle followed closely behind me as I pulled into the parking area.

He jammed his truck into park, grinding the gears and skidding to a halt, before he jumped out and started yelling. "Of all the stupid, no good, idiots—"

"I am not an idiot." I was full on sobbing at this point. "I was chasing a murderer, and if you hadn't been sleeping, we might have caught him."

"Sleeping?" He approached me quickly. "Sleeping? You think I would sleep on the job?"

"It sure sounded like it when you responded on the radio." I took a step back and tripped on something.

When I looked down, a chill ran up my spine. A crumpled up pair of waders sat beneath my feet, exactly like the one I'd seen the man wearing in the Muddy Water Cove. The rubber boots at the end of the pant legs were completely caked in mud.

In an instant, my jumbled thoughts came together like the pieces of a jigsaw puzzle.

"You." I did a mental head slap. How could I have missed it? "But Luke said you had a solid alibi."

"I don't know what you're talking about." Kyle's eyes were huge and red and his face looked demonic in the overhead light.

"You're the Muddy Water Bandit. You—you killed Ronnie."

A small smile came over his face. "And what makes you think that?"

I looked down at the waders beneath my feet. "She saw you. She was telling the truth."

"Who saw me do what? No one saw anything." He took another step toward me. I had to do something. I pulled the pepper spray from my belt.

"You think that's going to protect you? You already sprayed me once and look how much good that did."

He was right. Aside from the red eyes, it didn't seem to have much effect on him.

"Vaseline. Works like a charm."

"How did you know I'd spray you?"

"Last night when you found me, you seemed only too ready."

"You were out setting traps, weren't you? You haven't been taking them up to the storage block. You've been reusing them."

"I think that's about enough out of you. I'd have let you turn in your badge and leave but you had to get smart on me."

He lunged with the speed of a rattlesnake and the strength of a gorilla.

I had no chance.

His hands were wrapped around my neck squeezing so hard I thought my eyes might pop out of my head.

I tried to scream, but air couldn't escape my lips. I kicked at him, but it was no use. If only I could get to my radio. I reached up and grasped at where the mic sat on my shoulder.

The red emergency button was within my grasp until Kyle threw me to the ground. He ripped my mic from my hand and pulled the radio from my belt. I scrambled away from him resisting the urge to rub my bruised neck.

My phone. I had to get to my phone. I reached for my pocket but it wasn't there. Had it fallen out?

I stood and made a run for Cherry Anne when Kyle reached into the bed of his truck.

Ten feet.

Five.

Two.

I stretched for the door handle but came up short—something rough closed tight around my windpipe. Rope. Probably the same kind of rope that killed Ronnie.

The circulation in my face cut off. Darkness closed in on my vision as I clawed at the rope trying, and failing, to get my fingers between it and my skin.

He would stuff me into a trap like he had Ronnie. My mother would feel so guilty that we hadn't made up. She'd cry over my lifeless, bloated body.

And Luke, I should have texted him back.

Nikki would probably laugh and think good riddance.

And Antonio—Antonio was . . . there.

Wait, what?

My body fell to the dirt, my vision spotted and disjointed. Air rushed back into my lungs, burning, and I felt like I might pass out.

Someone—Antonio—had Kyle on the ground, trying to wrestle the rope from his hands.

I tried to sit up, tried to help, but my vision was closing in. Antonio wasn't winning, but he wasn't losing either. He almost had Kyle pinned when the world went dark.

I woke up with a killer headache to a sterile scent that reminded me of the time I'd gotten my appendix removed.

The hospital.

My hands went to my neck where they found soft bandages. I was alive.

I looked around to find my mother resting in a chair in the corner of the room.

"Mom?" I croaked out.

Her eyes fluttered open. "Rylie? Oh sweetheart!" She hurried over and scooped my hand up in both of hers. "I'm so sorry we fought."

"No, Mom, I'm sorry. I should have never—"

"Don't," she interrupted. "I almost lost you. If it wasn't for that co-worker of yours, I might have."

"Antonio." The memory of him and Kyle wrestling flooded back to me. "Is he okay?"

"I am fine," the Italian-laced voice said from the doorway. "And I'm happy to see you're okay too."

"Thank you. Thank you so much for saving me." Tears welled in my eyes. "How did you know?"

Antonio looked down at his feet, the first bit of insecurity I'd ever seen on him. "I was so stupid. I vouched for him, but I didn't know, I swear. If I had, this might have never happened."

"What are you talking about?"

"Kyle was supposed to have been at my party the night of the murder. I thought he was. I told the *police* he was. But then tonight when his wife told you he'd gotten the flu . . ." He rubbed a hand over his face. "I never should have left you with him but it was so hard to believe he could be a murderer."

"It's okay. At least you came back." I smiled. "But why murder Ronnie?"

"Kyle's an obsessive fisherman. He's been fishing the reservoir since it opened, since they introduced catfish. He's studied all the techniques, tried every single bait and lure and rod and he still couldn't catch the state record."

"Then Ronnie caught it." I nodded. Man, fishermen really were nuts.

"And Ben kept pulling up all those traps. Kyle was going berserk. All this time, I thought it was because we weren't getting any closer to catching the MWB." He shook his head.

"So what happened? How'd you beat him?"

Antonio puffed up his chest. "Well, I had him pretty well pinned when Luke showed up."

"Luke? How did Luke know?" My throat hurt when I talked.

"I called him when I couldn't focus on the game because I was so worried about you, and he met me at the reservoir. I'm just glad you were at the shop. Otherwise we may not have found you in time."

"And Luke is—"

"I imagine he's booking Kyle as we speak."

At least Carmen would be happy.

"I think that's enough for now." Mom cut in. I was silently thankful.

"That's okay. I should probably get home anyway. I'm glad you're okay." I don't know whether it was the fact that he saved me from near death or that he was just *that*

194

handsome, but when he smiled at me before walking out the door, my insides turned gelatinous.

"Well, he certainly is a very handsome gentleman," Mom said when he was gone.

"A very *married* gentleman," I replied.

To which she wrinkled her nose. "Too bad."

My thoughts exactly.

16

They kept me in the hospital overnight for monitoring but let me go home the next day. My neck was bandaged so the rope burn could heal, but otherwise I was apparently in perfect health.

"Luke's coming to visit in about an hour, if you want to get spiffed up," Mom informed me as we pulled into the driveway.

"Great," I replied, trying to keep the sarcasm from my voice. I was glad he had helped Antonio, but I didn't really want to see him after I knew he'd been with Nikki.

"Do you need any help?"

"No, I'll just throw on some clothes and swipe on some mascara."

"And do something with your hair. It's a mess." And just like that, my mom was back.

Luke and I sat in silence at the dining room table. He ran his fingers through his hair, and I tapped my freshly broken fingernails on the table.

"I'm glad you're okay," he finally said.

"Me too. Thanks for helping Antonio."

The look on his face at my mention of Antonio was almost enough of a payback for his willingness to date the vilest girl in the world. Almost.

"When he called, I dropped everything and got there as fast as I could."

I just nodded.

"You know, me and Nikki—"

I held up a hand. "You don't have to explain yourself. She's a beautiful girl. And you and I are just . . . friends."

He frowned but didn't contradict me. My heart squeezed a little at that. I sort of wished he had.

"I tried to call you, to check up on you," he said.

The memory of my phone buzzing in my pocket rushed back to me reminding me I'd have to somehow come up with the money for yet another new phone.

"I was busy trying to stop a killer."

"And stop him you did."

I nodded.

"I should probably go, let you rest."

Every part of me wanted to grab his hand. To cry on his shoulder. But he didn't need to be my fixer. Some things, I was just going to have to learn to handle on my own. "Thanks for stopping by."

The moment the door closed behind him, I dissolved into tears. Mom, who had likely been eavesdropping, plopped into the chair where Luke had just been and pulled my head onto her shoulder. "It'll be okay."

Maybe living at home wasn't the worst thing ever. Maybe.

A week later, I arrived back at the shop where I'd nearly died, dressed in my uniform and ready to return to work.

"It's good to have you back," Ben said. I thought he might hug me, but he didn't. "I'm glad you didn't quit."

"Quit? No way." Though the thought had crossed my mind, especially with Nikki working there.

"Great! And maybe this time you'll get the full-time position. I, personally, am hoping they pick you."

"What full-time position?" I'd been off painkillers for a solid three days, but my brain still felt a bit fuzzy.

"Kyle's. We'll need to fill it by the time summer's over. Just promise me you won't find any more dead bodies." He winked in the most big-brotherly way possible.

"Trust me, I'll be happy to put the dead bodies behind me."

Another full-time position. My heart raced. This was it, my chance at a fresh start.

That position was mine.

THANK YOU FOR READING
CATFISHED

I would be honored and eternally grateful if you would post a review on Amazon and/or Goodreads about the book.

Also, I love hearing from readers! Email me at stellabixbyauthor@gmail.com and sign up for my newsletter at www.stellabixby.com for exclusive content and up to date information about upcoming books in the Rylie Cooper Mystery Series.

XOXO,

Stella

ACKNOWLEDGMENTS

There are so many people to thank. Wow.

I must first thank God because He has given me every bit of ability, talent, perseverance, and grit I have. Without Him, there would be no me.

A very close second goes to my family. You are my heart and soul and I love you with every fiber of my being.

Nolan, you are my rock, the love of my life, and my best friend. Thank you for always seeing the best in me and believing I can accomplish anything I put my mind to, even when I don't. Your support of my writing has made all the difference. I thank God every day that He gave me you.

Faith, thank you for every single smile and word of

encouragement that you so freely give. I can't wait to read the book you bring to the world someday.

Lily, thank you for cheering me on in a way only you know how. Your constant outpouring of love and praise gets me through even the toughest of chapters.

Grant, thank you for being there every step of the way with this book, buddy. I couldn't have done it without you . . . literally.

Dad, thank you for being one of the first people to read CATFISHED. The day you asked to read it and the day you finished and told me how much you loved it were two of the best days ever. Your support means more to me than I can describe.

Mom, thank you for not only asking about my book but really listening to all that I have to say, which is a lot. Smile. Thank you for being my biggest fan.

Keri, thank you for calling me every. single. morning. Since the moment you were born, we've been the best of friends— minus my "take her back" moment, sorry about that—and I wouldn't have it any other way.

And to the rest of my family, thank you. You mean the world to me and I can't wait to hear what you think of the book.

Jenny, that cover, wow. Thank you for taking my vision and creating something beautiful.

Bethany, thank you for whipping my book into shape. Your editorial help was invaluable.

Michele, thank you for being one of the first people to encourage me to write and for inviting me to join WFTJ. I am eternally grateful.

WFTJ friends, you made me smile and got me started. I miss our Broadmoor dates!

Shawna, thank you. So. Much. I couldn't have asked for a better friend and mentor.

Brittany, I so appreciate your friendship and for getting me excited to write again.

Muddy River and Write On friends, thank you for reading my work every month. Your feedback and friendship is invaluable.

To all of my alpha and beta readers, Dad, Brittany, Matthew, Sue, Geniene, Emily, and Shawna, your feedback and cheerleading made a huge impact on this book and my ability to get it out into the world. Thank you and I hope you'll read book two!

To all of my ranger friends, though this book is fictional, the heart behind it rests in one of the best jobs I've ever had with some of the best people I've been privileged to know. Thank you for your friendship.

To all my early reviewers, whether you gave this book one star, five, or anywhere in between, I am so grateful that you would spend your time reading the words I've poured so much into. Keep doing what you do. You are important.

And last but absolutely not least, thank you to every single person who reads this book. I hope you like it and will read book two when it comes out!

ABOUT THE AUTHOR

Stella Bixby is a native Coloradan who loves to snowboard, pluck at the guitar, and play board games with her family. She was once a volunteer firefighter and a park ranger, but now spends most of her time making up stories and trying to figure out what to cook for dinner.

Connect with Stella on Facebook, Twitter, and Instagram @StellaBixby.

Stella loves to hear from her readers!
www.stellabixby.com

CPSIA information can be obtained
at www.ICGtesting.com
Printed in the USA
LVHW02s2115160518
577405LV00003BA/593/P

9 780999 602102